Claimed by the Bear

A Book in the Deerskin Peaks Series

Book One

J. Raven Wilde

Other Books by J. Raven Wilde

Standalone Novels

His Orders

Hot and Steamy Series

In Hot Pursuit

Hot Rod

One Hot Weekend

Falling For Series

Falling for the Rancher

Falling for the Cowboy

The Mummy's Curse Mini-Series

The Mummy's Curse Vol 1

The Sorcerer's Curse Vol 2

The Curse of Anubis Vol 3

The Mummy's Curse Mini-Series Box Set

Sanctuary Series

Claimed by the Alpha

The Omega and the Witch

The Rogue and the Rebel

Deerskin Peaks Series

Claimed by the Bear

Taming the Wildcat

1

Misty

She couldn't stop looking in the rearview mirror. Misty knew she should stop. It was a little ridiculous. Fifteen hundred miles was far enough, wasn't it? Without seeing a single set of headlights following her for more than two hours, she should've been relaxed, but she wasn't. Not yet. She didn't know for sure if she was safe yet—not with Lyle. He had really done a number on her, and she hated him for it. Her fingers tenderly touched her cheek. It still stung.

Misty kept trying to convince herself Lyle hadn't seen her leave. The man had no idea which direction she had gone. She had done an excellent job of not using any of her credit cards so there wouldn't be a paper trail. She hadn't told a single person where she was going or how long she would be gone. Well, except Amber and her bestie wasn't about to rat her out to the man who had put her in the hospital more than once. Lyle had nothing to go on. She had packed a bag and left.

She shouldn't be this worried still, but she knew why she was. Lyle was far darker than she'd ever imagined and far more deranged. He'd fit in perfectly with a dozen Lifetime movie roles as the spurned boyfriend turned murderer. She shivered thinking about that.

Better to think about something else.

Eyes itchy and dry, Misty realized she'd been traveling for almost twenty-four hours without a break. Her arms and shoulders ached from anxiety and tension, stress taking its toll on her body. She was road-weary, and another yawn sapped her will to go on. Any rational person would find a cheap roadside motel and snag a room for the night, but not her. Misty knew she was going to need sleep, her body and mind rebelling against her will, but she kept seeing him breaking down the door and dragging her by her hair to his waiting car. She didn't like thinking about what might happen if he got her back home. She didn't like thinking about that at all.

Misty knew it was irrational, but she couldn't seem to deny the fears.

She shook her head to stay awake, sleep doing its best to seduce her. Twice, she found herself steering the car back into the lane because she had drifted off, the Mini Cooper finding its way into the breakdown lane.

Catching a glimpse of a gas station off the next exit, she took the off-ramp, and a few turns later, she pulled into the parking lot, picking a spot around back. Shutting off the engine, Misty pushed the door open hard enough to make it bounce back in her face. Glad no one was around to notice, she sighed. How had she let herself get into this mess? Getting out, she stretched, hands reaching for the heavens, relishing the delicious pops along her spine. It always felt so good when her back did that.

Misty walked to the women's bathroom door, her heart dancing with an uneven beat, her hand hesitating as she reached for the knob.

Was he going to be waiting inside?

She knew it wasn't possible, but it still took a moment to convince herself of that and turn the knob. After using the bathroom and splashing water on her face, she felt slightly refreshed and happy Lyle wasn't hiding in a stall, waiting for her. Chewing the inside of her lower lip, she realized she didn't have any weapons. She hadn't even thought to bring the Swiss Army knife she had bought when she went camping with Amber one year. Misty had never even used the thing, but it would've given her some piece of mind to have it with her.

Coming back outside, Misty felt the weight of the miles on her. She was tired. Too tired. Her legs were rubbery, and her balance was off walking to the car. She shouldn't be driving since it hard to concentrate. Misty thought about the 5-Hour Energy drink and knew it wouldn't do any good. Her body and mind were rebelling. They'd had enough.

The driver's seat was anything but comfortable to sleep on, but it was the best she could do. Her Mini Cooper was partially hidden from view; any passing traffic was unable to see much of her between the dumpster in the parking lot and the corner of the building.

Locking the doors, she leaned back against the headrest, wanting to sleep for a few hours before hitting the road again. Misty hoped her mind would let go of the fear and anxiety and just let her get some much-needed rest. She didn't have to hope for long. Her deep, even breaths steamed the windows up, and she twitched, fighting off the memory of Lyle as sleep took her hostage.

2

Misty

Almost twenty-four hours earlier…

Misty stared at the tacky clock her boss had picked up from the Sharper Image catalog—as if it would buy him style points. It wasn't going to help. He was an idiot.

Exhaling, she squirmed in her chair, the thong reminding her of what was to come. She always felt so dirty wearing one. The fact she had lingerie on under her conservative, off-the-rack, casual skirt and blouse kept giving her heart a little pinch of excitement. She was never this adventurous.

The teasing bit of fabric gently rubbed in just the right spot. She was about to lose it. The seconds felt like minutes. When was this day going to end?

"Come on," she whispered, teeth clenched, the staccato tapping of her manicured nails drumming out a pattern on the desk.

Her heart pounded harder at the thought of what awaited her at home. Biting her lip, she squirmed again, relishing the dampness between her legs. Recently, she had decided to let her ex-boyfriend back into her life. It might not have been her finest hour, but hey, a girl had needs, right? Lyle had begged her until she finally relented and asked him to go out. They'd been seeing each other for over a month now, and the sex had been incredible.

He had been the one who told her to wear sexy lingerie under her work clothes, so she'd think about the two of them together all day while she worked.

He'd been right.

It was all she could think about.

She imagined his mouth against her throat, tongue teasing her skin, his hand moving between her legs, and her breath coming faster. Clenching her legs together, she uttered a soft moan. Her face flushed, and she glanced around, hoping no one had heard. Misty had to keep it together, but it was so hard. Her heart pounded in her ears as her breath came a little quicker. Lyle had also told her he had a surprise waiting for her.

She couldn't wait.

While Lyle was never very good at surprises, she was eager to see what he had in store. Toys? Role play? Oils? All of the above, please. She wondered if her coworkers realized how much she thought about those things. Misty doubted it. They all saw her as just a lowly administrative assistant, one step above the coffee girl.

Misty pictured Lyle when she was walking into her apartment. What would his surprise be? She'd figured out how to read him long ago. He always tried dropping hints without letting her in on the secret, but somehow managed to blow it. No, he wasn't good at surprises. But other things? Oh, he was definitely good at those.

Misty's sex tingled at the thought of the pleasurable things to come, and her body electrified, she couldn't help but smile. She needed to be touched, to be taken, to be had. Lyle never failed to satisfy her naughty side.

Their relationship was always rocky, but the sex, especially the makeup sex, was incredible. She hadn't had to use her little helper in the nightstand over the last month since they'd reconciled.

"Come on, come on," she begged the overpriced clock.

And then, the unthinkable happened

Her heart skipped a beat with the first ring of the phone, line one flashing at her.

No, no, no, no.

Even though her title was administrative assistant, she was, in reality, a glorified customer service representative. Misty looked around as she cautiously turned down the ringer volume. Part of her wanted to answer the godforsaken thing. It was her job, after all, and she enjoyed what she did. Most of the time. But damn, if she answered it now…

She shifted her legs and gasped in surprise, shocked by how wet she was. Misty couldn't answer the phone, not when she had a Lyle surprise waiting for her. If she answered, she'd be stuck. It would probably be one of those "forever" calls, the ones that took way longer than expected.

And besides, she was so, very horny.

Her eyes darted back to the stupid clock. "Come on."

Ten.

Ring.

She nearly jumped out of her skin, realizing she had turned the ringer up and not down. Misty almost knocked the phone off her desk, trying to turn it down before someone noticed.

Too late.

Her eyes met those of her by-the-book-supervisor. She was an angry stump of a woman, who spent most of her day perched in her office doorway eyeing the stable of cubicles, just hoping to swoop down and catch someone doing something they shouldn't be.

Wonderful.

Nine.

"Just hurry up." She exhaled dramatically.

Ring.

Eight.

"Misty." The diminutive woman was loud, a garish ball of negative energy with rainbow-colored hair, and a perpetual foul mood always permeated the air around her.

Seven.

"Yes, ma'am?" Misty said between clenched teeth, knowing what was coming.

"Is that your phone ringing?"

Six.

Some of her fellow cubicle denizens turned her way. Her face flushed. She hoped they couldn't tell how turned on she was. Or did she? The thought of them knowing made her heart flutter, her legs clenching closed to put more pressure on her clit. Quietly, she gasped.

Five.

"Did you not hear me? I asked you a question." She exhaled so loudly it sounded like a horse snorting.

Four.

"Are you ignoring your calls? You are still on the clock, Misty."

Her tone was sharp, leaving a bitter taste in Misty's mouth as she clenched her jaw. Misty could feel everyone's eyes staring at her now. If she had the guts, she would put the little toad in her place. But instead, she slowly picked up her headphones.

Ring.

Three.

"If you don't pick up the phone right now, I'm going to write this up, you know. You'll be docked pay."

Ring.

Two.

"My back is really bothering me today, and I'm just anxious to get home and take care of it. I see the heating pad in my future," Misty said, hoping she sounded convincing.

One.

Misty reached for the phone's receiver, willing it to stop ringing.

And then, mercifully, before she could pick it up, the ringing stopped.

Off the clock. At last.

Her coat was a swirl of green and blue, a coat hanger barely remaining upright, as she pulled it free. Slinging it over her arm, she rushed out of her workspace. She could feel her supervisor staring bullets at her, but the only thing she could think about was Lyle's dick.

Thick.

Swollen.

Dripping.

With snow still on the ground, she carefully walked across the street to the liquor store to grab a bottle of white wine and a one of red.

First, we drink, and then...

The overly crowded subway could not move fast enough. Visions of Lyle's tongue teasing her to ecstasy, and her body writhing in the throes of passion filled her head. Misty was so deep in her thoughts she was unprepared when the train jerked suddenly. She held onto the pole, but still bumped into the man behind her.

"Excuse me," she said, trying to avoid his eyes while her body tingled with desire for Lyle.

Tall and thick, the man looked like a football player with his wide shoulders, and his expansive chest filling out his suit nicely. She could easily see his thick biceps bulging, and his hands were like baseball mitts. Misty wondered what they would feel like against her body.

He smiled pleasantly, his eyes dancing to her breasts as their bodies jostled against each other. "Pardon me."

She looked away as the train pulled into the station right before her stop. Misty felt the pressure of the man's groin pressed against her backside, and butterflies fluttered beneath her heart while desire flooded her mind. The train took on even more passengers, their car becoming overcrowded forcing them to stay close together. It took every ounce of control not to press back against him with more pressure. She longed to be filled, her heart hammering and her fingers tingling at the prospect. Misty wanted Lyle, but she was so turned on by this stranger.

She started to move away when she felt the man's bulge twitch. A rush of excitement moving through her, she remained where she was. The doors closed, and when the train lurched forward, he rubbed up against her. Arching her back, she pressed her ass firmly against him.

Misty could tell he was getting aroused and was quite surprised by how turned on she was feeling from how hard he was. She leaned back against his growing bulge, letting there be no doubt what she wanted, but instead of reciprocating, he cleared his throat and apologized before moving away.

She felt slightly embarrassed, her body defying her. Her voice seemed lost, and Misty refused to make eye contact. She had never done anything so bold before. That just wasn't like her.

The train slowed as her station approached. She glanced at the man and caught him looking at her. He smiled as the train braked to a halt. She gave him a quick wink before darting out the door.

3

Misty

Her apartment building was just two blocks from the station, and her body thrummed with what she knew was waiting for her. Her nipples rubbed against her lacy bra and her thong teasing her, she was a moving flow of desire. She looked up at her apartment as it drew near, her heart thumping madly in her chest.

Lyle wasn't perfect. In fact, most of her friends said he was an asshole. But he was her asshole, and lately he had been so good. A year ago, he had cheated on her. The memory gave her pause as she hurried up the steps to the door, her heels clicking. He had been defiant in his reaction when she had confronted him.

"You fucking spying on me?" He had reared back, his hand cocked and rage in his eyes, a moment before she landed hard on the floor, her cheek on fire. His hand was still raised, and she cowered, begging him to leave, fear swelling her heart.

He did but not before he yelled, "I'm the best thing you ever had! Don't you ever forget that! No one wants you, you orphaned piece of shit."

A week later, he had asked to come back, but she had said no. The cheating had hurt bad enough, but his reminder she had no family was almost worse.

Then, three weeks later, he had called her and caught her at a weak moment, and she buckled. She couldn't help it. He could be so damned charming when he wanted to be. Lyle had come home and reclaimed her— mind, body, and soul. He'd used her so completely that night her body had ached with it for days. That sweet soreness from being taken by him still made her heart skip a beat.

So, as a reward for his redemption, she had wanted to celebrate with him. As she stepped off the elevator to her apartment floor, she couldn't help but smile.

Everything was perfect!

Happily, she slipped the key into the lock, the bolt sliding out of place. She gently closed the door behind her, locked it, and then set her shopping bag on the table. What was his surprise? She looked around quickly but didn't spot anything she'd consider surprise-worthy.

She was too aroused to put the parcels away, giddy about what was about to happen. She slipped off her shoes and tiptoed through the dining room on the way to the bedroom. No foreplay tonight, baby. It was on.

She shed her work clothes along the way, leaving just the lingerie, and stopped to admire herself in the floor-to-ceiling mirror on the dining room wall.

The gray bra, panty, and garter belt set was a great contrast to her tan skin. Biting her lip, she shivered with anticipation. Her pert breasts were cupped beautifully in the bra, and she couldn't help but touch herself through the soft cotton, her fingers finding her sensitive peaks.

She moaned, a rush of excitement raging through her, and a moment later, she heard another.

Only this time, it wasn't hers.

Misty cocked her head, carefully walked toward the bedroom, and froze. She bit her fist to keep from screaming, horrified by the salacious sounds filling her ears.

She couldn't believe it.

Lyle was having sex with another woman in their bed. She shivered, but this time it wasn't from arousal. Her mind raced, trying to make sense of what she was seeing. Misty stood by the open door, and the woman jumped, when she made eye contact with her, trying to get out from under Lyle. Lyle held her in place, pinning her arms to the bed and kept thrusting. It was creaking with each thrust.

Misty screamed in anguish, "Damn it! Get out!"

"Come on, baby, just relax. Let's have a threesome."

"A what? Fuck you!" Feeling completely overexposed in the lingerie, Misty went from shocked to mortified. "Get out now!"

"Oh, please, Misty. Get in here and see how good Destiny feels."

Destiny? What is she, a stripper?

"This has got to stop. Get out. Leave! Now!" The bed continued to creak, Lyle smiling, his eyes alive with a light Misty didn't care for at all. His hips kept flexing, thrusting against Destiny. She felt sick to her stomach and folded her arms across her chest.

Lyle jumped up, his engorged cock bouncing from the motion, and stepped toward Misty. He didn't say a word. He lashed out with a backhand that made Misty's teeth click together, and she bit her tongue. Her ears rang as she brought her hand up to her face.

"You don't tell me what to do, you stupid bitch. I brought Destiny home to spice up our love life."

"Guys, I think I'm just going—" Destiny said as she balled up the sheets—the ones Misty and Lyle had bought on sale together at Macy's—to cover herself.

"Shut up, Destiny," Lyle said, not taking his eyes off Misty.

"Lyle, you need to leave now." Misty's voice sounded weaker than it had a moment ago, and her legs shook.

"Stupid selfish bitch." Lyle shoved her into the wall. "Don't you realize we're not going to make it if we can't fix our intimacy problems? We need this. I need this. Or we're not going to make it."

And there it was. It was always about him.

"I don't want to sleep with a woman." Her voice was a whimper, jaw aching from where he'd hit her.

"Please. Your body was made to be with another woman."

What does that even mean?

"Just go. Please, Lyle. Just leave."

"Not happening, babe. No can do. See, you're not running things in this relationship. Not anymore. Things are getting stale. You're boring in the sack. Talk about a snooze fest. Why can't you get it through your head?"

Tears scampered down her cheeks, each one filled with regret. Why had she thought taking Lyle back was a good idea? Was she that naive? Was she that desperate?

"Just go."

"You always break up with me, but you come crawling back begging for it, don't you? You have nobody. You'll always take me back."

"Destiny, get dressed. We're getting a drink."

Lyle got dressed slowly, making sure Misty saw his manhood and his muscles rippling like waves beneath his skin with each movement he made.

Jabbing a finger at her, he put his arm around Destiny before saying, "And another thing. We're getting some drinks, but when I get back, you better be in a good mood and have dinner ready or there'll be consequences. Not the good kind. Got it?"

She nodded, sniffing loudly, hating herself for believing. Hating herself for hoping.

4

Tate

He threw the coiled ropes in the back of his Bronco, making sure to miss his shirt. The ropes were filthy after an afternoon rock climbing with two of his friends, and he didn't want to ruin the only clean shirt he had. Pretty pathetic a grown man had let his laundry go long enough to have only one clean shirt, but that was the truth.

"Tate, you coming over for the game tonight?" Jack sounded so hopeful, like always. Tate felt bad canceling at the last minute, but he just wasn't in the mood. He wanted to work out and pick up the lumber he needed to add on the screened-in porch to his cabin. Anything to keep busy. He just didn't want to be in town tonight. There were too many ladies trying to hook him up with their niece or sister or themselves. Not that he didn't enjoy a good game of mattress tag every now and then, but it was getting old. The town wasn't very big and people talked. He didn't need any static.

"I don't think so. I'm worn out."

"Come on, man. Supposed to be a good one."

Tate didn't even know who was playing. He wasn't really into watching sports. Now, playing them? Definitely. When he did go watch sports, he really just went over to be social. Tate realized being Sheriff was more than just arresting people and enforcing the law. It was also about connections and relationships between the townspeople and himself.

"Tell you what."

"What?" Jack asked, an edge in his voice as he put his climbing gear away in the back of his pickup.

"How about I bring some pizza over this weekend and you supply the beer?" Tate grabbed his shirt and then shut the tailgate.

Jack seemed to perk up hearing the offer of pizza. He smiled. "Sure. Sure. That'll work."

"All right. Good climbing today, Jack."

"Yeah, it was. I found a spot up north for our next adventure."

"Sounds good. I'll see you later."

"Later."

Tate climbed into his Bronco and headed back to town with the windows down and the radio on.

5

Misty

Misty stared at the pasta, stabbing at it periodically with her fork, eyes filled with anger. Lyle hadn't noticed and continued to shove forkful after forkful into his mouth like a feral cat. How could he stuff himself after cheating on her? Better yet, why had she cooked for him? Maybe Lyle was right and there was something wrong with her.

Although his infidelity had bothered her in the past, this was the final straw. There was no coming back from this. Their lease was up in two weeks, which was perfect timing. She would finally leave his sorry ass. Misty had been considering renewing the lease for another year, but after tonight, there was no way in hell she would even think about it.

She had to get out.

She had to get out now.

*****

Misty was doing the dishes, while Lyle was out drinking again, leaving her alone with her thoughts. Someone was knocking loudly on the door across the hall. It went on for over ten minutes before she sighed and went to look through the peephole. Her heart went cold.

"Misty! Open up!"

Lyle was drunk and pounding on the wrong door.

Stepping out into the hall, she got his attention. "Lyle? You're at the wrong apartment, dumbass."

He turned, hand still on the door for balance, and looked at her. Lyle was a complete mess.

"Drunk enough to pound on the wrong door for fifteen minutes. You're all class, Lyle. All class."

"Shut up," he hissed, his breath reeking with the stench of vodka and cigars. He stumbled past her into their apartment and fell on the living room couch.

Enough was enough. The moment Lyle passed out on the living room couch—like a dead sardine—Misty made her move.

She quietly packed an overnight bag, taking the one hundred eighty-two dollars in cash she kept in the coffee can on top of the fridge, and left. Misty didn't even bother to shut the door, much less lock it. With any luck, someone would come along and slit the bastard's throat while he slept it off.

Alone on the bustling streets of the New York suburbs, Misty called the only person she could think of for help— Amber, her ride-or-die since childhood. Amber's midnight Mustang made record time and pulled up to the curb while Misty was sitting on her overnight bag.

"Need a lift, stranger?"

"How'd ya know?" Misty tried a smile, but it didn't last.

"Get in. Let's blow this town."

They drove for a few minutes in silence, the music so low on Amber's radio Misty couldn't tell what song was playing. Thankfully, Amber broke the odd silence.

"You need to get away from him. Far, *far* away." Amber said. "Leave the sucker for good. You've been naive enough to stay with him after he cheated the first time. You'd be a damn fool to stick around now."

"You're right. But where would I go? My lease is up soon, and I don't have another place to stay."

"I'd let you crash with me, but I have a better place in mind." Amber smiled, a sly look on her face. "My dad has a cabin in Wyoming. Real quaint. Out in the mountains with woods all around. He used to go up there for hunting, but he hasn't made the trip in years. I can loan you a car and you can take a little vacation for a few weeks. You certainly need it after tonight."

"I don't know." Misty hesitated. She was never this impulsive. "Do you really think running away is a good idea?"

"You're not running away! You're taking a break from all the stress. All the Lyle-ness that's built up over the last year. It's a break and a well-deserved break at that."

"Fine." Misty finally agreed. "Maybe you're right. Maybe this will be good for me. I've always wanted to go camping, you know."

"It's not really camping. It's a cabin with water, electricity, and a roof. It's not like I'm giving you some ratty old tent and a compass."

They laughed together. Amber was always good to her.

"Fine. I'll go."

"Perfect!" Amber did a happy clap. "This is a fresh start for you as a single woman, Misty. Now that you're back on the market, Wyoming better watch out!"

6

Misty

After being away from Lyle for seven days, it felt good to be on her own, making strides to better herself. She was sick of putting up with Lyle year after year. The feeling of leaving, with no intention of turning back, was oddly liberating for Misty.

Granted, the first night wasn't the easiest of her life. She'd been too afraid to check into a hotel and had just hidden behind a gas station. For some reason, she kept worrying about Lyle finding her. There was no way he was following her. How could he? She was using cash and was staying off the main highways whenever possible. There was no way he knew where she was going. Lyle barely knew Amber, and even Misty hadn't known about the cabin.

She was feeling so good. After a solid week of relaxation. As odd as it sounded, erasing her iPod and loading it with new music had been cathartic. She'd excised all thoughts of Lyle. At least most days she had.

As much as she loved Lyle, the events from last week were unforgivable. Being caught with another woman under the thinly veiled pretense of arranging a threesome was a new low, even for him.

Driving had always been a therapy of sorts for her and this time had been no different. She hadn't been in any hurry, taking nearly a week to drive to the cabin, each day a gift. She hadn't been on her own in almost five years, and it was heaven. Worries about Lyle, her stupid job, and the lease had all faded with every mile she traveled, closing the gap to Deerskin Peaks.

The woodland roads and secluded forests, surrounding her, as she closed in on the cabin, were so peaceful. With the windows down, the crisp, mountain air whipped through her dark-brown locks, and tickled her nose with the saccharine scents of firewood and fir. The music blasting in her ears was loud enough to drown out any lingering thoughts of Lyle, her iPod offering the same solace it had so many times in the past. Misty made a mental note to block Lyle's number when she got to the cabin. The last thing she wanted was for her serenity to be ruined by him.

Misty pulled up to the cabin just as the sun was beginning to scrape the horizon. She walked through the weathered door, into the cabin that looked like nobody had been there in months. A thick layer of dust coated every visible surface, and it smelled stuffy. Cobwebs dangled from the ceiling like silk chandeliers. Misty knew it would take some serious work, but she was actually looking forward to it. Keeping her mind occupied would do her body good. Hands on her hips, she thought about going into town to pick up the necessary cleaning supplies. A sneeze snuck up on her, the dust thick in the air.

After leaving Lyle last week, she'd made sure to clean out her savings and checking accounts. She wasn't stupid. Misty knew Lyle would try to find her. Taking everything with her in cash would prevent him from tracking her through her debit card usage. She didn't think he was necessarily going to give up so easily. A fish hook of worry tugged on her heart, but she pushed it away, not letting emotion get the better of her. Misty realized, she should've left Lyle a long time ago.

Opening a few windows to air out the place, she decided the cleaning could wait. She'd take a short hike instead. She hadn't driven God knew how many miles just to waste a beautiful high-country sunset. Being immersed in nature would be soothing, perhaps even spiritual. Misty looked forward to the enveloping night when the sky overhead would be strewn with constellations.

As she plodded through the overgrown grass, the trees thick around her, snapping limbs echoed around her. Curious, she moved in that direction, spotting a bear in the distance. At first, fear tickled her heart and her breath caught in her throat. Misty was surprised by how big he was, his form immense, as he moved slowly through the trees. His brown fur was in stark contrast to the vibrant greens of the forest. For a moment she worried what the bear might do if it saw her, a smile flickering across her lips. She figured if she could put up with a wild animal of a boyfriend for as long as she had, she could handle a bear.

Too tired to keep hiking, she admired the bear a few moments longer before turning back. The sound of him rending bark from a tree echoed through the forest around her. His fur was a magnificent shade of brown, light like a caramel apple. Misty caught herself smiling at the sight. It was beautiful. So much for a zoo when you could see wildlife up close.

7

Tate

The morning was chillier than it should be. He groaned. He'd forgotten to close the window again. His shoes and socks were on the other side of the room. The hardwood was going to be like ice. He took a deep breath and wrapped the comforter around him. Tate stood and immediately regretted it the instant his feet met the frigid floor. Why hadn't he installed the furnace last summer? He'd talked about it. He'd even priced it, but he never bought it.

He walked across the floor, grabbed his shoes and socks, and muttered on the way to the chair in the corner.

After getting dressed, he closed the window and thought about his day. Marty was off, so it just left himself and Murray on shift. It was going to be a really long day, and he still needed to pick up some things on the way to work.

8

Misty

The next morning was chilly. The cabin only had a fireplace and a wood-burning stove. Tugging on a hoodie, Misty decided to head town. Unless she wanted to inhale year-old dust bunnies the entire day, she needed to get supplies to clean the cabin.

The drive down the mountain to town was beautiful; the sun danced through the branches, splashing across the road in bright swatches of light. It only took ten minutes to get to town. A quaint town square was ensconced at its heart with a movie theater and flower shop nearby. It took her a few minutes to find the Oak Supply Closet convenience shop farther down the block.

Bells on the door jingled jovially as she stepped inside. Misty picked out the cleaning supplies with the funniest names, not sure what would work best. Toilet Extravaganza Bonanza sounded dangerous, but she would take a chance on it, and she couldn't resist Willy's Wood Shiner just on the name alone. As she searched for a broom, the leaves on the porch coming to mind, a gruff man with a muscular build stepped in her way. He didn't smile, his eyes intent on something behind her.

"Excuse me," he said curly. "Sheriff coming through."

"Oh, sorry, am I in your way?"

"No, but I'm just in desperate need of some Clean-and-Wash." The man pointed at an ugly brown stain on the front of his uniform. "I had a fight with my coffee this morning and lost."

Misty grinned, the sheriff returning one of his own.

"Going to have any scars?" Misty asked.

He chuckled, teasing her to giggle, and she took stock of his physique as he moved down the aisle for the stain remover. He was at least six feet tall, and his uniform was snug around his impressive pecs and toned biceps, his bulging muscles clear to see beneath the thin fabric. Despite the coffee stain, he looked handsome. His beard was trimmed, and his cropped brown hair was styled in a way meant to look strategically tousled. His chocolate-brown eyes looked like they could melt even the coldest soul. Misty's eyes lingered on the sheriff's impressive form as he walked away with his bottle of sacred Clean-and-Wash.

Damn. His wife was one lucky woman.

9

Tate

Tate had never expected a simple morning run to Oak Supply Closet to turn into a macrocosmic revelation. He had been to the quaint convenience store more times than he could count and seldom experienced anything even remotely exciting while shopping there. After all, it was a rickety old shop on the outskirts of town, limping along for longer than anyone could remember. Yesterday had been the exception. He wondered if she would be at the shop again this morning.

Tate stopped to pick up a couple sodas and granola bars when he caught the lingering scent of something so alluring a simple whiff was enough to send his senses into overdrive. Tate instantly recognized it as the natural odor of the woman from yesterday. He hadn't gotten her name but could picture her beautiful face vividly.

As he continued to covertly sniff around the aisles, Tate's inner bear instincts kicked in. The woman's heavenly smell amplified as he made his way to the checkout counter.

Could she be in the shop somewhere? Perhaps she had just left and I'm smelling the remnants of her scent.

Tate's nose tingled with every breath he took.

She must be close.

Too distracted to give the cashier the correct change, Tate made a beeline for the front door, stumbling backward as the very same woman entered the shop. She seemed startled by his presence, his lumbering frame towering over her, like a bear about to pounce. His senses tingled, he took in her scent once more and politely stepped aside so the woman can enter. "Sorry," he muttered.

"It's okay," she replied, flashing an uneasy grin. "Haven't I seen you before?"

"Yes, in this very shop. Yesterday in fact," Tate said, suddenly nervous, adjusting the collar of his uniform. "My name's Tate."

"Misty." The woman outstretched her hand. "Nice to meet you. Or re-meet you, I suppose."

"Likewise." Tate tried his best to control the animalistic fire burning within, his inner bear yearning for her. He needed to leave before his arousal was noticed. Nodding, he made his way back to his car, his two sodas and granola bars in hand, and his mind spiraled out of control.

There was something about Misty's scent unlike the scent of any other female he'd encountered before. Despite her timid nature, her scent was warm and inviting, like a gentle fireplace whose flames remain steadfast even in the dead of night. Bear shifters' heightened sense of smell allowed them to glean things from scents regular humans could not. Tate wondered if Misty was meant to be his soul mate. Every bear shifter had one, and he had yet to find his. Could it be this chance meeting had happened for a reason?

Tate had never been drawn to someone so strongly before. As he made his way to work, he concocted a plan to get close to Misty without scaring her off.

*****

After his shift, Tate walked through the woods to Misty's cabin; his cabin was less than a mile away. He was drawn by her unmistakable fragrance and had come without his uniform to be less intimidating.

Immediately, he spotted her on the front porch, nestled on a wooden chair with an open book and a cup of coffee.

He approached slowly, the bear inside raging with a magnetic desire that took every ounce of control to hide. "Hey there!" he called out. "Misty, right? Is this where you're staying? My cabin is about a mile up the road. Just thought I'd go on an off-duty patrol and stop by to say hi."

"Well, in that case, hello!" Misty abandoned her book, stepping to the top of the porch steps. She looked so inviting with her hands clinging to the weathered wooden railing and her hair swaying in the breeze.

"Are you enjoying your stay so far?" Tate asked, trying to read Misty, her scent driving him mad.

"Seems nice. Secluded. Beautiful views. So, yeah, for the most part. I've got some cleaning to do." She gestured toward the cabin. "Been awhile since anyone has been up here."

Tate noticed the disorganized pile of logs by Misty's front steps. "Need help chopping those? I'm real handy with an ax, you know." He felt like an idiot offering something so stupid, but he couldn't think of anything else to keep the conversation going.

"I think I'll do it myself, but I appreciate the offer." Misty wrapped her arm around the railing post, cocking her hips to one side. Was she deliberately toying with him?

"Well, let me know if you ever need anything. I'd be more than happy to oblige, especially for a woman as stunning as you."

Now he sounded even dumber. Maybe he should quit while he was ahead. He was about to head back to his cabin when he saw Misty smiling. She coyly tucked a lock of hair behind her ear.

"You know, we're having an auction at the town hall tonight if you want to stop by. There's bingo too, if you're into that sort of thing. It's a charity event for a family who lost their cabin to a fire last month. It would be nice to see you there. Living in such a small town, I see the same ugly mugs every day."

"I'll think about it." She chuckled. "If I'm not too busy, I might be there."

"No pressure." Tate lifted his hands into the air. "But if you do show up, be prepared to lose. I'm a mighty fine bingo player. Skill. Pure skill."

She didn't say anything, and he was worried he'd worn out his stay, so he nodded to her. "Well, I don't want to bother you. Enjoy the rest of your evening."

"Okay. Thanks for stopping by."

He headed back the way he'd come, slipping between the trees. As he weaved through the lush mass of pines, Tate felt his bear senses kick in, stimulated by the environment. His senses told him Misty was closed off for a reason. She must have experienced some sort of recent heartbreak to be so guarded. Tate wondered if she had come up there to hide from someone or maybe get out of a toxic situation. Either way, he empathized with whatever Misty was dealing with and vowed to take care of her from afar. The bear inside of him was naturally protective. He hoped to take care of Misty as she worked through her pain.

10

Misty

Misty's heart swelled at the thought of being invited to a local event. As a foster care child who was constantly shipped from home to home, the fact Tate had gone out of his way to include her in something in town after only talking to her for five minutes touched her.

Although she was hesitant to mingle with a large crowd of strangers who likely all knew each other well enough to send around Christmas cards, she couldn't turn down his invitation. She didn't know any men like Tate. He was confident and humble at the same time. Respectful, kind, and dashingly handsome in one package was a powerful combination she didn't come across very often.

As the sun melted into a gilded sky behind the trees, Misty posed in front of the bathroom mirror. She had to get dolled up for bingo night. Applying a modest layer of makeup—"no one likes a whore," Sister Catherine's admonishment living on from her orphanage days—she styled her hair. She slipped into a cotton dress speckled with tiny daisies and paired it with a simple pair of ebony flats. She checked to make sure there was no hint of the red lace bra and panty set beneath. Lipstick dry to the touch and hair smoothed back in an elegant bun, Misty piled into her car and made her way into the heart of Deerskin Peaks, heart full of nervous energy.

Rolling up to a modest brick building lined with a worn wraparound porch, Misty found a parking spot. She locked the car as dusk tried to take the day hostage, and she admired the illuminating porch lights, their golden bulbs like fireflies on each cabin as far as she could see. A menagerie of trees and shrubs embraced the land beyond the heart of Deerskin Peaks, blending into a lush forest and rocky terrain. Misty couldn't help but smile at such a picturesque sight. Wyoming was more beautiful than she ever imagined. Perhaps she could find a way to stay a little longer, or even make it her new home.

Home.

She entered the town hall, an ensemble of friendly folks chatting over drinks eating greasy food, nodding, and waving. Tate noticed her right away and motioned to her as he talked with a gruff-looking man with a graying goatee. He waved to her and excused himself from his table, the man with the gray goatee following.

"You made it!" Tate exclaimed. He turned to his friend. "Jack, this is the newcomer, Misty. And Misty, this is Jack. He owns a bar and grill down the block."

"Is it called Jack's?"

"How did you know?" Jack asked, smiling.

"Lucky guess." She shrugged. "It's nice to meet you." Misty nodded at Jack, her eyes continually going to his goatee. It was a little out of control.

"Nice to meet you." Jack smiled back and shook her hand. "We have bingo every Tuesday and one charity event per month. I'm always here for the charity events."

Misty stared at Tate, Jack's words fading away. Tate looked delicious. His jeans were tight in all the right places, and his shirt was filled out by his wide shoulders. She thought he had cologne on but wasn't close enough to tell for sure.

An awkward silence stretched as Tate caught her looking at him, and her cheeks flushed. Clearing his throat, he asked, "What do you think of our little town so far? Oh, and where are you from, by the way?"

"Uh, well…" Misty's voice trailed off. How honest should she be? Did she really want them in her business? In the end, she decided it wouldn't matter. What would it hurt if they knew? "I'm actually from New York."

"Wow! Big city girl, eh? What brought you all the way over here?"

"Just needed a break." It wasn't a total lie.

"How long are you going to be in town?"

"I'm not sure. I thought it was just going to be a vacation, but now, I'm not so sure."

Tate gave her shoulder an affectionate squeeze. It made her wonder how it would feel to have those hands pin her down on the bed, their bodies writhing against one another.

"Well, whatever you decide, I hope you enjoy your stay. And like I said earlier, if you need anything, don't hesitate to ask. Just a phone call away."

Tate pulled out his cell phone and handed it to her so she could input her phone number. She let her hand brush his when she took the phone from him, and the electric charge of his touch was immediate. It had been a while since she'd had sex, and Misty was dying to be taken. She knew she'd have to take matters into her own hands if it didn't happen soon. Maybe later tonight, she'd have to light a few candles and put on some soft music, and enjoy herself with the two toys she'd brought.

She felt Tate staring at her and pulled herself from her thoughts. Misty wondered how long she'd been daydreaming about masturbating and if Tate could somehow tell what she'd been thinking. Keying in her number, she handed his phone back and folded her arms. At least she could reach him at the touch of a button.

Bingo lasted over an hour, and the two of them shared a large order of sweet potato fries. It was wonderful being with a man who respected her. Misty wasn't afraid of Tate. Oddly, she felt protected. Safe. They'd just met, but she trusted him. She'd let her guard down and relaxed for the first time since breaking up with Lyle. It was heaven.

"I've got a joke for you."

"Better be a good one," Misty said, eyeing him dubiously, as she used her dauber to mark off twenty-two on her card.

"Oh, it's one of my best." He breathed on his fingernails and rubbed them against his shirt, winking at her.

She realized he hadn't marked a single number on his card. "Then spill it, lawman."

"Why did the melon jump in the lake?"

He'd been focused on her, not bingo. She smiled. He kept making sure their elbows touched while they sat next to each other.

"I have no idea."

"Because he wanted to be a watermelon!" Tate said, barely able to contain himself, laughing at his own joke.

"Wow. One of your best?" She pretended not to like it, teasing him.

"Well, sure. What's not to like."

"It's terrible."

"No, it's not." Tate winked at her.

"It's like my coworker's son's jokes."

"How so?" Tate asked, elbow firmly planted in the middle of his card.

"He's in third grade."

"Oh, ouch. Hurtful."

"Got another one?" Misty asked, marking off another number. She had a chance for bingo in two different directions. She could use the hundred-dollar pot.

"Why are stadiums always so cool?"

"Stadiums?" Misty asked, waiting for the next number to be called.

"Yeah."

"I don't know. Why are they so cool?"

"Because, they're always filled with fans!" This time, his eyes came alive as he laughed, and she couldn't help but laugh with him.

"There's something wrong with you."

"Maybe."

"No maybe about it. Definitely something wrong."

"So, didn't like the second one either?" Tate asked, nudging her arm with his elbow.

"Fourteen," said the caller, an elderly woman in bad need of a makeover, her sweater from somewhere in the Clinton administration.

She daubed fourteen. She had bingo. "Bingo!"

The room filled with muttered curses. These people took their bingo seriously.

Tate stood up and took her card.

"Hey, wait. What are you doing?" Misty reached for the card but Tate playfully slapped her hand away.

"Have to check the card." He fanned the card at her.

"Oh."

Her face was probably ten different shades of red, and a few people nearby chuckled. How did she not realize what he was doing? Was she that desperate to win the money that she actually thought Tate was going to try to collect it? She was an idiot.

A moment later, the caller said, "We have a winner. We have bingo."

Tate walked back with an envelope in his hand, tapping it against his temple. "This contains the secret to all your woes."

"Woes?"

Nodding, he handed her the envelope.

"Who are you?"

"Batman. But don't tell anyone."

She laughed out loud, his response catching her off guard.

An older woman with glasses dangling from a chain around her neck tried to shush her.

"I think I should call it a night. I kind of think I'm not exactly their favorite person at the moment."

"Oh, it's just Dottie. Now, Dottie, would you please stop harassing the young lady. If you don't watch it, I'll come ticket you for too many tomato plants."

Dottie scoffed and turned away.

"Thanks for inviting me. I'll see you later." Misty stood, Tate following her to the door.

"It's barely ten. Why don't we make a quick stop at Jack's place? The bar and grill are open until midnight, and if you don't mind a little ptomaine poisoning, Jack makes a reasonably tasty burger. You barely touched your fries. Need to eat something."

"I guess so." Misty chuckled not realizing he was watching her so closely. She wasn't exactly crazy about sweet potato fries but hadn't wanted to seem rude. "Jack's place it is."

They walked the block and a half to Jack's. Most everyone they passed seemed to be staring at them. Was it because Tate was the sheriff? Did they want to know who the new girl was? She saw the sign for Jack's, an illuminated playing card poking out of a beer mug.

"I was like you, you know. Deerskin Peaks was just supposed to be a short layover, a place to earn a few bucks before moving on—at least that's what I told myself—but this place got its hooks in me, and here I am."

He held the door for her, still talking and they walked inside and found a corner booth. The décor was quaint; antiques adorned the walls, and chandeliers made out of deer antlers, their light dim, hung from the ceiling.

"I grew up in Nebraska with my grandparents and worked their farm, but when my grandma died when I was twelve, my gramps was too feeble to care for me, and I was forced into the foster care system."

"I'm sorry to hear that." Misty wondered if she should tell him she was a foster kid too as a young waitress with an array of facial piercings and spiked blonde hair put two water glasses on the table.

"How are you two doing this evening?" the waitress asked.

"Doing all right, Lizzie. How about you?" Tate leaned back in his seat.

Lizzie's eyes darting between the two of them. "Just fine. Who's your new friend?" She pulled out a pen and battered pad of paper for their order.

"This is Misty. She just came to town a few days ago."

"Well, what do you think of our little slice of heaven?" Lizzie's tone was full of sarcasm.

"It's just what I needed. Quiet. Slow."

"Oh, it's got that in spades," Lizzie said, nodding.

"She's from New York City." Tate smiled at Misty and she hoped she wasn't blushing too much.

"Now that's a drive. How long are you staying?"

Misty shrugged, a sigh escaping. The sixty-four-thousand-dollar question. "Not really sure. Just taking it day by day."

"Well, don't take it too many days; this town has a way of brainwashing you until you don't know any better and you think it's perfect, and twenty years later, you realize you've been stuck here with no prospects and nothing to show for your trouble."

Misty was at a loss. She didn't know what to say.

"It's not all bad," Tate said, winking at Misty.

"Not all good either," Lizzie said. "What would you guys like to order?"

Tate motioned to Misty who glanced at the one-page menu. "Uh, let's see. I guess I'll have the club sandwich and fries. Can I get a Coke to drink?"

"Sure thing. Tate?"

"I'll have the steak sandwich with fries and a Budweiser. Bottle if you have it."

"Medium rare as usual?"

"You know it." Tate smiled gathering up the menus and tucking them behind the caddy with mustard and ketchup bottles.

"Have this up for you guys in a few." Lizzie spun on her heels and made her way through a swinging door to the kitchen, leaving them to stare at each other for a few moments before Tate continued his story.

"So, where were we?"

"Foster care," Misty said, taking a drink of water and wincing at the metallic taste.

"Right, right. Well, at first, I was really mad at my grandpa. It felt like he was abandoning me, you know? But as I got older, I understood. Anyways, I moved around a lot as a teenager. I was in a different foster home every month. I never thought it was gonna end." Tate was quiet, absently tapping his fingers against the worn tabletop. "But when I was sixteen, I finally caught a break. Whether it was God showing mercy or just stupid luck, I don't know but I was finally placed with a nice family who treated me like one of their own. I got to do football, track, you name it. After I graduated high school, I went into the military. I traveled all over the world with the army, and that's how I met Jack. The two of us became inseparable, and he convinced me to move here with him after our eight-year stint was over. And well, here I am a hundred years later."

"I was a foster kid, too." Despite being such a naturally private person, she was warming to Tate more quickly than she'd expected. She trusted him to hear her story, but she wasn't quite ready to tell him about Lyle yet. "I was left as a baby and never met my birth parents. I looked for them a lot as a teenager but never found anything. Like you, I had a hard time growing up. I'm doing all right for myself but I've always felt like something was missing. I've always longed for a family…a family of my own."

"You'll find what you're looking for," Tate assured her. "I can promise you that."

Lizzie brought their plates, but Misty barely noticed. She was completely enamored with Tate. And though she didn't want to get in a relationship—chaos still ransacking her heart after Lyle—she saw the signs.

Did he feel the same?

Misty only paid attention to the conversation, which was funny and light and Tate. When he smiled or laughed, his crow's feet feathering at the edges of his eyes. His reassuring tone and intense way he listened to her every word was perfect.

The staff started sweeping the floors and putting the chairs up on tables. The time had slipped by so quickly Misty hadn't realized it was almost midnight and the staff at Jack's was preparing to close.

Tate smiled at her. "Didn't realize it was this late."

"Me neither."

"Why don't I walk you to your car. You okay driving the mountain pass in the dark?"

Scooting her chair in, she wanted to say no. She wanted to have him drive her home, come inside and seduce her. Misty could easily imagine his firm body drawing her to his, her hands exploring his muscular form, feeling his excitement growing. She felt the familiar tingle between her legs and wished Tate was inside of her. As much as she wanted it, she knew it would be a mistake.

"I'm fine." But she was anything but fine. She wanted him to use her until her body ached with it. She wanted to feel the wave of sweet exhaustion, the sheets damp with their sweat, and his body slick against hers.

Standing next to her car, Tate stepped in and gave her a hug, his arms enveloping her. She breathed in his musky cologne, and the spikes of his beard tickled her cheeks and neck. Misty yearned for the moment to last forever, a time capsule in her heart. She had never met someone who excited her body and her mind so much.

*****

Back at the cabin, the night was painfully slow. After tossing and turning in the cabin's creaky twin-bed, she pounded the pillow as if it was the reason she couldn't sleep. The hands on the clock made their way to three in the morning, sleep a pipedream.

It wasn't that she couldn't get comfortable; it was sprinkled thoughts of Lyle poisoning her with insomnia. He'd managed to needle his way into her thoughts, and she hated him for it. This was supposed to be her haven, her safe harbor where all things Lyle weren't welcome.

Frustrated, she sat up with her legs off the edge of the bed and her feet touching the hardwood floor. She regretted it immediately. The floor was freezing. Tucking her feet into fuzzy slippers, she went to the bathroom and splashed some water on her face.

You're letting him win, again. He's not worth it. No more.

Looking at her reflection, water dripping from her nose and chin, she noticed the circles under her eyes. Damn you, Lyle.

Defeated and exhausted, Misty slipped back into bed and finally drifted off to sleep. Instead of Lyle tormenting her, it was Tate teasing her body to ecstasy, each caress arousing her to new heights.

11

Misty

The dawn was still painting the sky when Misty began her day, walking down the porch steps to the tangle of loose wood against the front of the cabin. Channeling her anger toward Lyle from the night before, she eyed the ax. She'd never used one before, but how hard could it be?

The idea of a raging fire crackling away as her mouth explored Tate's taut body fueled her despite her apprehension. After placing the first log on the stump, she took a long drink of her coffee, hoping the caffeine would finally kick in and scare the cobwebs away.

Taking in the tranquil view, she cupped her mug with her hands and let the warmth seep into them. She loved the way the pines swayed in the gentle wind, whispering among themselves in a language only they knew. The stream looked beautiful as it cut between dozens of boulders, a silvery ribbon of motion, bubbling and brewing like a crystalline witch's brew.

Taking another sip of her coffee, she put it down on the bottom step, the stack of wood calling her name. Misty adjusted the piece of wood and set her feet, her hands finding purchase along the smooth ax handle. She had no clue what she was doing and hoped she'd hold on to both feet before it was all said and done. Hefting the ax above her head, she brought it down in a neat arc, the head of the ax neatly biting into the wood. Smiling, thankful she hadn't chopped off anything she needed, she tried it again. This time, it bit a little deeper, but she still failed to split the log. It was harder than she'd thought it would be. The movies always made it look so easy.

Twenty minutes later, breathing hard and her shoulders aching, Misty wondered if she would ever split the damned log. She was definitely not pioneer material.

She lost her temper, and Lyle slipped into her thoughts, his mocking tone, his smug look. He had always told her she was worthless. Unable to take care of herself. Misty didn't want him to be right.

Rage fueled her arms, the anger warming her. Misty began to swing wildly, the ax head bouncing off the log again and again. Twice she knocked the log off the stump and had to reposition it. Misty wasn't going to give up. Lyle wasn't going to be right.

Fifteen minutes later, the log still mocked her. It was chipped with sections of bark missing, but it still remained intact. The adrenaline racing through her body made her hands tremble and her legs weak. Emotion stalked her, wheedling its way into her heart. The memories of the previous evening were lost on her as she struggled to fight back the tears.

Maybe Lyle was right.

Here she was, alone in the woods, unable to split a single log. The tears were warm against her cheek, the morning sun spilling across her upturned face. As she sobbed, the ax dropped to the ground.

Even thousands of miles away, Lyle still managed to control her. Why did he have this hold over her? She'd managed to push him from her mind for a few days, but here he was again, stomping all over her heart, his words like daggers. The heartless bastard was still stirring her thoughts into a swirling mess.

Would she ever be free of him?

Not liking the way she was feeling, she sat on the step and finished her coffee. Not even the sun could burn away the dismal thoughts haunting her.

12

Tate

Tate was enjoying the crisp air of dawn when he heard a woman sobbing nearby. Was she hurt? Where was it coming from? Lumbering through the brush, his massive paws pounding the soft undergrowth, he was every bit of his bear counterpart, his full transformation complete. Following the familiar scent, he closed in on the sounds, a cabin coming into sight. He recognized it and moved closer still, cautious and concerned.

A moment later, he saw Misty sitting on the porch steps crying, and his heart ached. Had something happened to her?

He wanted nothing more than to break through the tree line and hold her, soothing her aching heart.

Concentrating a moment, he considered approaching her. Even though he was in bear form, she would know it was him. He could let her know his secret and bring her fully into his world. He decided against letting her see him.

Moving closer to the cabin, he noticed the ax on the ground, a single log resting on the tree stump. He was about to say something to her when she flew into a rage, screaming to the forest around her, wielding the ax like a madwoman.

He stopped mid-stride, watching her swing wildly again and again, the ax head not hitting the log square, glancing off over and over. The ax fell to the ground as she sobbed. She sat back down on the porch steps, her hands cupping her coffee, the steam rising. She inhaled a shaky breath before taking a drink. His heart felt like it was held in a giant vise. He wanted nothing more than to run to her and hold her. It was an overwhelming desire, one he didn't fully understand. Watching her break down shattered his heart, but he knew he couldn't get closer in his current state.

Making sure he wasn't spotted; he made his way back into the woods and hurried to his cabin. Once inside, he transformed back into his human form. He knew what he had to do. After pulling on some clothes, he took a second to straighten his hair. For some reason, it was always a mess after he transformed back into human form.

Racing through the woods, ignoring the branches raking across his face, he couldn't stop thinking about her. She'd done nothing but poke her way into his dreams all night, her long hair teasing his bare chest, her bare breasts against his face, and her body writhing on top of his. He tried pushing those thoughts away knowing it wasn't what she needed right now, but it was hard.

A moment later, he broke into the clearing around the cabin, heart stumbling in his chest, his mind awash with thoughts of Misty in his arms. He and his bear were worried about her.

She was still crying, but at least she wasn't sobbing uncontrollably anymore. The log was off the stump and the ax was at her feet. He wondered about his course of action. Was she going to be startled he was there or would she welcome him? Tate hoped it was the latter. Eager to lend a hand, he nervously moved closer, rubbing his hands up and down on his thighs.

Tucking his hands into the back pockets of his jeans, he cleared his throat so she'd hear him. She turned quickly, eyes wide, surprise etched on her face. Looking down, she dashed away the tears.

"Tate? I didn't expect to see you this morning." Her voice was filled with surprise.

"I was just out for my morning walk and heard some noise over this way. I was worried something had happened so I thought I'd come over and check it out." Tate didn't want to embarrass her and didn't mention the tears still drying on her cheeks.

"I'm sorry. Just having a pity party. Had some bad dreams last night and thought I'd get an early start on this stupid wood but it's a lot harder than I thought it would be."

He nodded, folding his arms, and put one foot on the step next to Misty. It was hard being so close; her scent was strong, its affect instant. "I'm sorry about the bad dreams. I have those nights too."

She looked skeptical, so he thought he should take a different tack, picked up the ax, liking its weight in his hand.

"I'm just having a bad day."

He didn't make a comment, and brought down the ax in a quick, practiced motion, the log splitting neatly in two, falling to the ground. Picking up another log, he smiled at Misty.

"Show-off."

Tate thought she was joking but was having a hard time reading her. "You just gotta get the hang of it. It takes time and practice, just like anything else."

"Right. Practice." She looked down into her coffee mug.

This wasn't going how he'd planned at all. He felt his nerves tugging at his resolve. "Hey, I could teach you how it's done if you want." His smile wavered and then faded as she shook her head, putting her mug down on the step.

"Thanks, but no thanks." Misty wiped away the tears with the collar of her pajama shirt. "I'd love to learn, but now's not the best time. My heart's not in it right now."

He took another log from the pile and split it neatly. Tate had to keep his hands busy, nervous energy nipping at him.

"Is something wrong?" He chopped another log neatly in half before picking up another one. "Do you want to talk about it?"

The silence was agonizing, but he knew he couldn't force her to talk. He split four more logs as Misty seemed to be finding the courage to tell him what was bothering her. Tate just kept working, knowing she'd find the words when it was time.

The pile of split wood began to grow before she cleared her throat, rubbing her hands along the outside of her legs. He realized she was still wearing slippers. It made him smile. Chopping wood in bedroom slippers. Only a city girl would even try.

"Well, here's the thing," Misty finally said, her voice still tainted with emotion. "I lied to you about why I came up here."

He hadn't expected that.

"I didn't really come up here for a vacation. Not even close."

Tate nodded, stacking the wood he'd split alongside the cabin.

"I didn't sleep well last night because my asshole ex-boyfriend…" She took a deep shuddering breath and cleared her throat. "He's actually the reason I came up."

"To clear your head?"

"Yeah, I mean, I guess. I don't know. I just needed to get away from him and his stupidity. I guess I was hoping for a fresh start and all. We'd been together for over a year. We'd had trouble, breaking up more than once before getting back together. Stupidly, I took him back, and last week, I caught him in our bed with another woman. Nothing like getting smacked right in the face by your boyfriend's infidelity, right?"

Her smile was shaky, but at least it was a smile.

"I can only imagine."

"Well, it wasn't the first time he cheated. He'd done it right after we started dating too. This time he tried to play it off like he was trying to set up a threesome but I'm not an idiot. He acted like I was crazy to not want it. The bastard didn't even stop fucking her while he was talking to me. What the hell is that?"

She shook her head, waving her hands in front of her. "Well, that was it. I was done being taken advantage of and basically decided to call it quits. For good this time. I don't want anything to do with him. Even though I'm glad to be out of such a toxic situation—and believe me, it was definitely toxic—he still messes with my head. I hear him reminding me of all my horrible qualities, telling me I'm useless. I know it's not true deep down, but sometimes it still gets to me."

She stood up, leaning against the railing lining the steps, fidgeting with her fingers. He wanted nothing more than to hold her and soothe her aching heart.

"Lyle sounds like a real prick. I'm glad you're far, far away from him." Tate felt his anger flare, and his cheeks flushed with the inner rage building. It took every ounce of control to not turn into his bear form, find this Lyle, and shred him to a bloody pulp.

Granted, even though he wasn't part of the relationship and he didn't know everything that had transpired, for Lyle to have treated Misty so cruelly was uncalled for. Even though they had only met two days ago, Tate could sense Misty was an incredible person. She was much more than Lyle claimed, and for him to not see it was a perfect reason for her not to stay with him. She was not only beautiful, but she was incredibly sexy, alluring in a way he'd never known before. If Lyle was blind to it, he didn't deserve her in the first place.

"Me too." Misty sniffed loudly. "Sorry, my nose is a mess with crying and everything. You know, sometimes I can't believe I put up with him for so long. I mean, I've been here for, like, forty-eight hours, and you've treated me better than he did the entire time we were together. How ridiculous is that? On our first date, we went to Olive Garden of all places. I'm not into Italian at all, but I didn't want to be rude. Besides, Lyle was cute in a bad boy kind of way. I hadn't dated all that much and figured what the hell. So, Lyle showed up twenty minutes late and didn't even pay for our dinner."

"You have to be kidding."

"I'm not."

"That's awful." Tate swung the ax again and split another log. "I guess he never learned how to treat a woman right. What a jackass. I mean, being punctual for a first date is just common sense, isn't it? It's about respect. Your time is just as important as my time. That should've been your first warning sign. Should've cut and run right there. Maybe snatch up the breadsticks on your way out for your trouble. I mean, you can't go to Olive Garden and not have the breadsticks."

Misty began to giggle before sniffing again. "You're right on that one, I suppose. Are there any Olive Gardens around here? Maybe we can go sometime."

"I would love that, but I didn't think you were an Italian girl?"

"Oh, I'm not entirely. According to an ancestry test, I'm Irish and Italian."

It was his turn to laugh. "Nice. But seriously, I didn't think you liked Italian food."

"Oh, I don't, but they have a mother of a salad."

"That's true. Very true." He smiled, his heart warmed by Misty's words. He wanted nothing more than to shift into his bear form and roar with all he could muster at Lyle's mistreatment of Misty. How could he have done those things to her? How could anyone? He would have to be content enough knowing he at least got Misty to smile.

"But getting back to your main point. It's still his loss. He treated you like shit, and now he's paying the price. Fuck him if he doesn't get it. He doesn't deserve you. And you're better off without the son of a bitch."

"Trust me, I know. But toxic or not, breakups still suck."

"Amen to that."

Despite the lighthearted turn in their conversation, Tate still stewed with anger over Lyle. Although he had never met Misty's ex, the way she described him made it blatantly obvious Lyle was nothing but a cruel-hearted person without an ounce of compassion. He'd been a festering wound on Misty's heart long enough, a poison tainting Misty's sweet soul for far too long.

His mental abuse was bad enough, but then he cheated on her without even trying to hide it. He had no respect for himself, her or their relationship. It was clear he'd worn down Misty's mental state to a point where she'd been broken. The more he thought about it, the more Tate's inner bear clawed at his insides, desperate to make an appearance and go on a rampage. At times like these, being a bear shifter was more harmful than good. If Tate didn't have his bear under control, there was no doubt he'd be shifting in public, right in front of Misty's eyes. Perhaps there would be an opportune time to tell her in the future, but right now, Tate couldn't risk exposing such a secretive part of himself when Misty was still dealing with so much. Explaining that he was a bear shifter would surely scare her off for good.

As he finished off the last of the firewood, Tate promised to make sure Misty would someday realize what she was truly worth. He'd do whatever it took for her to see herself the way he did, and if taking down her bastard of an ex-boyfriend would help in that endeavor, then God help Lyle.

13

Misty

Misty was still down in spite of Tate's efforts earlier. She shook her head as she realized she'd just wasted twenty minutes staring out the kitchen window at the beautiful view. A part of her wished Tate was part of that view and he could've stayed the entire day to help her forget about Lyle, but she knew he had a job to do and simply couldn't waste his time on her and the mess she was in. Even so, releasing all the pent-up resentment rotting inside her about how much of an asshole Lyle was had felt strangely therapeutic.

Despite being so upset, Tate's physique hadn't been lost on her. She'd loved watching Tate's biceps bulge and swell as he worked through the wood. His immediate support of her was heartwarming, and a smile flickered across her lips. The way he talked shit about Lyle without a care in the world was a nice surprise. It reminded her of high school with two boys fighting over her. It was an unexpected pick-me-up to an otherwise dreary day.

Misty poured a second cup of coffee and she thought of him swinging the ax, as her own personal Paul Bunyan. Why had she been so resistant to have him show her how to chop wood? She apparently had no problem watching him do all the work she'd wanted to do.

When she'd first met Tate, she'd been aroused, and who wouldn't have been? But she had assumed that was all it was. Animalistic attraction. She had tried to dismiss it as just that, but it was harder to do than she wanted to admit. At first, she dismissed the giddy rise of emotions whenever Tate was nearby as nothing more than being aroused by human contact. After all, Misty was holed up in a secluded cabin in the middle of Wyoming's densest forest.

However, the more she thought about it, the more Misty realized it wasn't just lust. Her feelings ran far deeper than she'd initially thought. Misty was falling for Tate. She longed to have another display of his rippling muscles and his handsome face. She wanted to run a hand through his brown hair and feel his prickly beard tickle her face as she kissed him. Misty ached for a man to touch her. She wanted to smell him on her after they'd finished, the delicious musk following her the rest of the day. More than that, she wanted Tate to be her refuge from the malignant thoughts she was having about Lyle because she knew Tate was the only one who could console her. Lyle's voice had returned with a vengeance the second Tate disappeared back into the woods, and Misty hated it. If Tate was still there, he would tell her Lyle wasn't even worth the time and he was better off with whatever bimbo he had chosen over Misty anyway. She tried to make herself believe it, but it was hard to do.

To distract herself, Misty took out her phone to call Amber. She had one bar, and she hoped it would be good enough to at least complete the call. The reception in the woods wasn't the best, but she hoped it would let her talk with Amber.

"Hello?" Anber answered.

"Hey, Amber. It's Misty."

"Misty, oh my gosh. Hi!" Amber's energy was always infectious. Misty couldn't help but smile as Amber rambled on, not letting her get in a word. "I was just thinking about you this morning, actually! How funny is that? How are things out there in the great wild yonder? Are you enjoying the cabin? Have you seen any mountain lions or wild animals yet?"

"I'm doing all right, and no, I have not seen any mountain lions, thank God. I did get to see a bear though. I really like it here. Compared to New York, this place is so quiet and quaint, you know? I can see the stars at night for the first time. Back in the city, there's way too much smog. You can't see anything but the moon and sometimes not even that."

"Tell me about it." Amber replied, chuckled. "I'm glad you're settling in, though."

"It's been an adjustment, but this place is just what I needed. This place needed some serious scrubbing when I first arrived. I honestly wondered it was a shithole when I first got here. I thought what the hell you had gotten me into. But I've cleaned it up since then. Plus, the town sheriff has been stopping by to help too. He's really nice."

"Town sheriff, eh?" Amber scoffed, her tone clear and suggestive. "You sure he's *just* coming over to help?"

"Yes, yes, I'm sure. As cute as he is, I'm not sure if I'm ready to move on after Lyle so soon. I don't know. One crash and burn per year is my limit. Feeling a little gun-shy at the moment."

"If you feel a spark, then go for it, girl." Amber giggled. Just sleep with him. You probably could use a little stress release. Am I right? Besides, you're not getting any younger."

"Very funny."

"But anyways, I was actually thinking of stopping by to say hello. I have a seminar in Muskegon. It's like thirty miles from Deerskin Peaks. I fly in on Friday. Real boring stuff, but work is work. The good news is, the company is paying for the flights so, in a way, it's like a mini vacation. Or at least that's how I'm trying to see it. To be honest, anything far away from New York would count as a vacation."

"I'd love for you to stop by! I bet your dad would be really happy with how I've spruced this place up. If you want to spend the night, I can lend you the bed. I don't mind sleeping on the futon."

"We'll see when I get there. I appreciate the offer, though." Muffled voices shouted in the background. Amber yelled something indistinct back before returning to the phone. "I'm about to clock in for work, so I've got to go. It was really nice talking with you. I'll let you know when my flight lands on Friday, and we can sort out everything from there. Talk to you later, Misty."

Amber hung up before Misty could even say goodbye. Amber always was impatient. Misty smiled, excited about the upcoming visit. She'd have to pick up some beer and munchies to snack on. She wondered what kind of activities the two of them could do together, and she walked into the kitchen for a third cup of coffee.

To her dismay, the pot was empty, forcing Misty to seek caffeine elsewhere. She brewed a pack of green tea claiming to have just as much of a kick as regular coffee, loading her mug with both milk and sugar. No way could she stomach green tea straight.

Piping-hot cup in her hands, Misty decided to head back onto the porch to soak up the scenery again. She always felt more at ease outdoors anyway. When she opened the front door, Tate was standing there with his fist in the air, seconds away from knocking. Startled by his sudden presence, Misty gasped and nearly spilled her tea. Although she was excited to be in Tate's company, she was caught off guard, not expecting his beaming face to be on the other side of the door. Even so, she ushered him inside and invited him to stay for tea.

14

Tate

Tate hadn't intended to spook Misty. She was trying to play it off like she hadn't been startled, but he knew otherwise. Her scent had changed. It was much stronger because her heart rate was raised and her sweat stronger.

All he'd been doing was waiting for her phone call to end so he could knock on the door. Thanks to his bear-shifting abilities, all his senses were heightened. He'd clearly heard her conversation on the phone. He had no idea who she was talking to, but he'd decided not to interrupt when she started talking about the town and how she felt about him. He'd smiled when she'd said his name. It also stirred his desire to know she thought about him.

He'd been lost in thoughts when she opened the door, the same stupid smile on his face, standing there like an idiot with his fist up in the air. Given the circumstances, even he had to admit the situation seemed a little stalker-ish even without ulterior motives.

"Shit!"

"Sorry!" Tate exclaimed. "I didn't mean to startle you."

"You didn't. I mean, whatever. It's okay." Misty laughed and shook her head. "Bad timing is all. What are you doing back here so soon? Am I really that intriguing that you can't get away from me?"

"Admittedly yes, you are. But that's not why I'm here. I came to invite you to dinner. Tonight, at my place. I want you to see the sunset from my side of the mountain. It's lovely here—don't get me wrong—but there are too many trees in the way. My cabin has the best view in all of Deerskin Peaks."

"That's a bold claim to make," Misty said, a playful tone to her voice. She smirked. "But I'd love to come and judge for myself. Dinner at yours sounds great, especially since I have no food here anyway."

"Perfect. I'll pick you up at six. Sound good?"

"Sounds great." An ear-to-ear grin crossed Misty's face. Tate could tell she was more excited than she was letting on, which in turn stirred his inner bear. As Tate said goodbye and made his way down Misty's steps, Misty added, "I'm really looking forward to it. Have big shoes to fill, though."

Turning to face her, he asked, "What do you mean?"

"Well, you have me thinking about Olive Garden from earlier, and those are big shoes to fill."

He laughed. "Yes, those are. I'll see you at six!" Raising his hand, he headed back through the woods.

*****

The scent of grilled salmon freshly caught, filled his cabin, teasing his inner bear to make an appearance. Between the fish and Misty's scent comingling, his inner bear was fighting him tonight. Misty took a sip of the most expensive chardonnay the town had to offer.

She winked at him. "This is pretty good stuff. Local?"

He shrugged. Tate had no idea. He knew wine was white or red. That was the extent of his wine knowledge. He brought the plates over, salmon with green beans and rice filling them nicely.

"Looks wonderful." Misty smiled at him as he set her plate down.

"Looks can be deceiving."

She took a bite of rice and then of the salmon. "But not in this case." She smiled. "Why aren't you taken? Have a great job. I mean, you have job security like nobody's business. Crime, right? There's always crime."

"Not as much as you would think in this little town."

"Well, still. You're reasonably good-looking." A playful smirk tugged Misty's lips to one side.

"Ouch. Hurtful."

"Sometimes, the truth hurts." She laughed, and it teased butterflies into his stomach. He never wanted her to stop laughing.

They finished dinner and went into the living room, and Tate put one of his old records on.

"Boz Skaggs? Really?"

"Too cool for you, huh?" Tate teased Misty.

"Oh, definitely not cool enough for the Boz."

"I can put on something else."

"Oh, no, no, no. You have to stay true to your joy, misguided though it is."

Now it was his turn to laugh. "Would you like to sit out on the porch? I do believe the show is about to start."

They sat on the wicker couch. He deliberately took the end closest to the door because it had a few broken strands that always poked the backs of his legs. He didn't want Misty to have to put up with that.

Sipping wine and laughing together, they soaked up the magnificent sunset until it faded into the gentle velvet haze of nightfall. Their conversation never lagged. There were no awkward silences or strange pauses. Just words. Laughter. Tate felt completely connected with Misty and wanted to claim her as his own now more than ever. The bear inside him was longing for a partner as perfect as she was.

15

Tate

When their dinner date finally ended, Tate drove Misty back to her cabin. He realized how he felt and wanted to protect her. The woods were beautiful, but they were also deadly, especially at night. Mountain lions, wolves, bobcats, and, yes, even bears were known to roam the area. They pulled into the gravel area in front of her cabin. He almost hoped something would happen so he could demonstrate his fierce masculinity. Tate wanted Misty to admire his bravery.

"Dinner was really fun. That salmon was phenomenal. I can't believe you caught it yourself. Since when do you fish?"

"I'm a jack-of-all-trades," Tate laughed and shrugged off the comment. "But I'm glad you enjoyed it. I really liked the evening too. I like to think I'm the romantic type, but sometimes I worry the dates I plan end up being boring."

"Date, huh? Is that what this was?"

"It's whatever you want it to be." No longer able to quell his desires, Tate acted on impulse. He'd been dying kiss Misty since he caught her inviting scent at the convenience store, and now he had his chance. She smelled even more divine now sitting beside him in the truck. Leaning over, he kissed her passionately, cradling both of her cheeks with his hands. His heart exploded as he felt her soft lips against his own, her mouth opening to his. Losing himself in an ocean of lust, drowning in an animalistic heat, their tongues met, dancing with the moment. Misty retaliated by kissing him even harder, her hands finding his thigh. Her touch was like fire to gasoline, his passion igniting, and his cock stirred from the sensation. He couldn't help but cup her breast with his hand, softly squeezing, feeling her shudder with pleasure.

Kissing along her throat, Tate gently stroked her inner thigh, his mouth finding hers again. As she opened her mouth, she moaned, Tate kissed her deeply before pinching her lower lip between his teeth, softly biting. As he fumbled with the buttons on her jeans, she pulled away suddenly, lust in her eyes, passion moving through her.

"Is something wrong? Was the lip bite too much? I'm sorry for being so aggressive. It's just that—"

"No, no. Everything's fine. I really enjoyed that kiss. Like, a *lot*. But I just don't want to move too fast. We haven't known each other for very long and I'm still getting over Lyle." She ran her fingers through her tangle of mussed brown hair.

"No worries." Tate lovingly brushed a lock of hair from Misty's eyes. "I'll go as slow as you want me to. Whatever pace you need, I'm down for it. I don't want to push any boundaries. I just have never felt a connection like I do with you."

"Sounds a little trite."

"Trite or not, it's how I feel. There's something about you. You turn me on like nobody's business, but it's more than that. I love talking to you and love your laugh."

"Whoa, slow it down there, Tex. Let's put it in park for a minute, okay?"

"Sure, sorry." He smiled, clearing his throat, still feeling as if he'd done something wrong.

"Thank you. I appreciate you doing this." She touched his arm and gently squeezed. "A lot of guys just want to get in girls' pants and skip the whole getting to know them part. I feel the same things about you. I'm very turned on by you and love talking with you and laughing. It's almost too perfect."

He opened his mouth to say something but she held up her hand to quiet him.

"Not tonight, okay? But soon. I promise. I've really got to get some rest, but I want you to know tonight was one of the best nights I've had in a while."

He nodded and smiled. "I'm glad. Have a good night, Misty."

"You too, Tate."

She climbed out of his truck and then up the cabin steps. She turned and waved before disappearing into the cabin, closing the door behind her. Tate backed the truck into the mountain road, and he felt his bear stirring again, this time more restlessly. He wanted Misty as his mate more than ever before.

"Me too, buddy," Tate said to his inner bear sympathetically. "Me too."

16

Misty

It had been two days since she kissed Tate. Each day she spent without him was torture, but they had agreed to take things slowly for now and Misty wanted to respect their decision. Even so, sometimes she caught herself daydreaming of how blissful their second kiss would be.

The morning light was so breathtaking. Misty walked toward the cliff's edge to take in the impressive view. Another rustic town sprawled in the valley below, the high altitude making the buildings and people look like doll's toys. She'd have to ask Tate what it was called.

As she moved further along the edge, Misty thought of Tate, her heart scampered recklessly. He definitely made her tingle in all the right places. She closed her eyes and pictured what he might look like without his shirt on. Would he have a bare chest or a thick carpet of chest hair and rock-solid abs? She hoped it was hairy. The idea of running her fingers through it and feeling it rough against her bare breasts was incredible. It was no secret Tate was ripped, and with a body like that, Misty couldn't help but wonder how good he'd be in bed. She wanted it to be rough with his body firm and his hands hard against her body.

A noise startled her from her fantasy, and she saw a bear moving through the nearby forest. Although she had expected to run into smaller forest creatures—birds, squirrels, a racoon even—seeing a bear so close was nothing short of terrifying. She had spotted one on her second day at the cabin, but it had been at a much safer distance.

Misty knew better than to make any sudden moves, slowly inching her way back toward home. Her heart pounded away, and blood drummed in her ears. The bear roamed less than fifty yards away, unaware she was there. Despite that, she willed herself to be as quiet as possible, avoiding sticks and dry leaves. She didn't want to draw any attention to herself.

The bear looked in her direction, and she froze. He sniffed the air, his huge snout bobbing with the motion. Grumbling, the bear looked along the cliff edge, standing almost perfectly still like one of the carved bear figurines found at a rural hobby shop. If she wasn't so scared, Misty would've loved to get even closer. Its chocolate-brown fur and piercing ebony eyes, amazed her. It was definitely a creature of fierce beauty. Misty wondered if perhaps it *was* the same bear as before. The reserved way the creature stood resembled the body language of the languid bear she saw a week ago when she'd arrived.

As Misty retreated to a safe distance, she made a mental note to let Tate know about Deerskin Peaks newest resident. She didn't know if they would try to relocate him, but she thought they should know a dangerous predator was roaming so close to civilization. The last thing Misty wanted was to wake up to a bear on her doorstep.

*****

Misty made it home in under thirty minutes, glancing over her shoulder every few minutes to make sure the bear wasn't following. She peeled off her jacket and running tights and took off her baseball cap, hair tumbling to her shoulders. Glancing in the mirror, she posed, pulling her hair up and then letting it fall to her shoulders. She wondered how Tate would prefer it. Misty also wondered what color lingerie might send him over the edge. The familiar tingle was back, and she rubbed herself a few times between her legs, enjoying the pressure. Now wasn't the time.

But an evening of self-pleasure and pampering might not be a bad idea. It would at least get rid of the tension that kept building to the point she was worried she might attack Tate. She didn't want to do anything she'd regret later.

She poured a glass of the same wine she'd had at Tate's. She hadn't been lying when she told Tate it was good. Misty lit some pine scented candles and placed them carefully in the bathroom. She took another sip of wine before starting the tub, making the water almost too hot to stand. The clawfoot tub looked divine, with steam rising from it. After putting a stack of freshly washed towels on the closed toilet seat, she undressed. Her hands brushed over her nipples, the sensation impossibly arousing.

Misty slipped into her makeshift sauna. The steam, heat, and scented candles relaxed her. Closing her eyes, she thought of Tate again, her hand pausing between her legs and her breath catching in her throat. He really turned her on in the worst way.

Misty contemplated her relationship with Tate for what felt like the umpteenth time. Being one of the few people she knew in Deerskin Peaks, Tate had become her main source of socializing as well as the subject of her desire. It was a foregone conclusion. Her heart was completely his. They might wait a week or a month, but she was entirely his. Body, soul, heart, and mind.

She hadn't been in town long, and they were already incredibly close. Much closer than Misty would have ever anticipated. After their first kiss, she had made it very clear she wanted to take things slowly, the acrid sting of Lyle still fresh. She didn't think Tate was Lyle, but part of her was still healing. She didn't want to step into something potentially long-term with Tate if she wasn't ready. He was sweet and caring, but Misty didn't think he would be willing to play with an on-again off-again relationship. And she couldn't blame him. She didn't want that either.

Despite that, she wondered how long it would take for their physical relationship to overcome them both and extend beyond just kissing. She could tell how aroused Tate became just by being next to her. Misty knew it would be incredible when they finally took that final step.

Tate, had said he wouldn't go beyond a casual make-out session or the occasional kiss on the neck, and Misty was sure he would stay respectful of her wish to keep intimacy at a minimum. However, Misty could not deny the desire she had for him, and the draw was almost palpable. She had an insatiable desire to push the envelope and see what Tate was like in bed instead of simply dreaming about it. She had concocted so many arousing fantasies about his the daydreams felt more like memories. It was just a matter of time before they came to fruition. It was up to her to decide when.

Still deep in thought, Misty shifted her focus to the outfit picked out for tomorrow's date with Tate. The two of them planned to eat at Feathered Grouse, a well-established restaurant serving exotic and tender game. Sick of wearing outfits designed for a Catholic schoolgirl, Misty had gone into town the other day in search of a woman's clothing store, determined to spice up her wardrobe in preparation for the other kind of spice she was anticipating when dinner was over.

She found a sexy outfit cut perfectly to highlight her body's natural curves, teasing her cleavage with a low-cut vee in the center. She felt free picking out her own clothes, something which never happened with Lyle.

Afraid of attracting unwanted attention from wandering eyes when they went out in public together, Lyle always needed to approve her clothes before purchase. At the time, Misty had obliged, but now she was free from Lyle's toxic mess, she was starkly aware of how controlling his actions had been. Lyle had no right to dictate Misty's wardrobe. Sure, if it was something playful for the two of them in the bedroom, that might be fun—but not on an ongoing basis.

Knowing she was going to strut around town in something far too revealing for Lyle's liking felt oddly liberating. She was turned on by the idea.

17

Tate

Tate was dumbfounded. He'd found a poorly designed missing person flyer with Misty's beautiful face in the middle of it in his inbox. It was being sent to all law enforcement agencies apparently. The concerned boyfriend was eager to find any leads and was willing to pay for any information that led to her.

What an asshole.

Lyle's contact information was at the bottom of the flyer.

Just staring at the virtual flyer made Tate's bear stir with anger. He knew if Lyle took one step into Deerskin Peaks he'd be torn to shreds. It was instinctual. Tate knew Lyle was nothing but bad news. He wasn't going to stop until he killed Misty. Tate knew the type. Sad to say, it was an all too familiar story even out in the wilds of Wyoming.

Transforming into the intimidating protector of the forest and clawing away at Lyle's feeble body was something he could only dream of. But as much as Tate loathed Lyle's pathetic existence, violence was never his prerogative.

Tate signed out of his email before his rage consumed him and headed to the local bakery for some pastries for an after-dinner indulgence. As he drove through town, he wondered how Misty was doing. They'd been going on a lot of dates lately which was wonderful. He learned new things about her each time he saw her and looked forward to seeing her more often and gaining more insight into her personality. They had a dinner date planned for later tonight, and neither Tate nor his bear could wait to see Misty.

****

Dinner had been nothing short of exceptional, and with empty plates in front of them, they held hands across the table. Misty looked incredible in a tight dress leaving nothing to imagination. He had a hard time keeping his eyes from her cleavage. Tate had to keep adjusting the way he was sitting because his erection kept getting twisted in his underwear.

God, he wanted her.

"Do you want to pick up some dessert?" Tate asked, his hand reaching for hers, her touch always electric to him.

"I found a bakery the other day," Misty said, a playful tone in her voice.

"That right?"

"Want to pick up some pastries?" Her fingers teased the palm of his hand, driving him insane.

He had never been more aroused by a single touch in his life. "Sure. That sounds good."

They walked to the bakery, the night aging around them and the sun succumbing to the horizon in a blaze of furious color. He was more content than he could ever remember being, which was strange. Even though it was agonizing not to sleep with her, it was okay. He just loved being with her. In the past, he would've been aggravated if he wasn't sleeping with his girlfriend after the second date. But not with Misty. She was different. He was willing to wait as long as necessary. She was the one.

It took them fifteen minutes of giggling and joking around before they finally managed to fill a box with delicious goodness, the clerks obviously not impressed with their silly banter. They made it back to his truck and he unlocked the door, opening it for her.

"Milady."

"Why, kind sir, what wonderful manners you have. Your mother must be proud."

"I wouldn't know. I was raised by wolves."

"Indeed. How truly curious."

They laughed as he drove them back to his place, the headlights lancing through the darkness pressing in on the road. It didn't take long before he pulled into the drive of his cabin.

Once inside, he put on Boz Skaggs again. Again, Misty laughed at his record collection, but he didn't mind since it was all in good fun. In fact, it was one of his favorite things about Misty along with all the things she'd taught him like humility and to relax. She'd taught him more about himself than any woman had.

Sitting on the opposite side of the table, he opened the box, and they stared at an assortment of doughnuts before stuffing their mouths with everything from vanilla cream Long Johns to powdered doughnut holes. After a night of refined elegance and proper table etiquette back at the restaurant, sitting back and gorging on cheap pastries like savages was incredibly satisfying.

"Fried dough really hits the spot," Tate exclaimed, rubbing his stomach. "Especially after a giant slab of venison."

Misty laughed at him patting his stomach like Santa Claus after his harrowing Christmas Eve jaunt. Lying on the couch, he closed his eyes in a post-dinner coma. She took their plates and wine glasses to the kitchen.

"Hope you're in the mood for a little more fun than just eating ourselves stupid tonight," Misty said with a playful tone. "Because if you bail on me and pass out right now, I'm going to be very upset. It's only eight thirty. My carriage doesn't turn back into a pumpkin until one am."

"I thought it was midnight."

"I'm not Cinderella, dear, and I ain't got no fairy godmother either," he said, putting the plates in the kitchen.

He sat up, smiling. Tate loved when she was playful like this. "Well, it's a good thing you don't have a fairy godmother, or I'd have to tell her about you using your womanly wiles to try and seduce me after I bought you pastries no less."

"So, you're saying you wouldn't accept my womanly wiles as a generous gift for such a kind and gentlemanly man?" Misty laughed, rinsing the dishes before turning and facing Tate still lying down on the couch.

"I would indeed accept any and all gifts from my darling rainbow."

"Rainbow?"

"Yeah, I couldn't come up with anything else. My brain is on food overload. It's kind of sad really. I can't think straight."

"So, you can't add two and two?"

"Only if it equals six," Tate said, laughing at his own joke, massaging his temples with his fingers.

"And are you weak with a food overdose/"

"Yes." He wondered where she was going with this.

"Too weak to resist?"

He chuckled, turning to face her. "Probably."

"Good." Misty smirked. "Because I've been waiting to do *this* all day."

In one swift motion, Misty beelined back to the couch and planted herself on top of Tate's muscular torso with a feline elegance. With one knee nestled on each side of his rib cage, she brushed the hair from his face and leaned down for a kiss. The moment their lips touched, passion ignited them. Tate's drowsiness dissipated, his carnal desire returning, as he ran his hands over every inch of Misty's body.

"Not so tired now, are you?" she asked between breaths.

"I guess not. Something really woke me up. It was probably a squirrel in the chimney." Tate grabbed Misty's slender wrist and gently guided her hand down to his crotch. She massaged his big bulge, her hand moving like a metal detector searching for something valuable. She giggled, a playful sound, and broke free from his grasp. She pressed her warm palm fully against the thick fabric of his jeans and gently squeezed. Tate suppressed a guttural moan. This was the first time Misty had ever touched his cock, and he wanted to enjoy it.

"Let's pause for a second." She reluctantly pulled away. "Before we go any further, I have to use the little girls' room."

"Now?" Tate asked playfully. He thought they were going to go a lot further than they had. His cock throbbed, and his pants were tight. "Things were just heating up."

"Calm down. I'll just be a second." Misty hopped off the couch and tiptoed to the bathroom like a minx.

Tate groaned quietly and stroked himself to maintain the blood flow, not wanting his erection to die down before Misty came back. As he continued to stroke himself impatiently, his inner bear stirred once more. This time it was stronger, clawing at his insides like a ravenous, lust-filled beast. Tate did his best to quell the feeling, reminding his bear that it was still too soon. His bear had to be patient. The right time would come to introduce Misty to his bear. He hoped she'd welcome him in either form. The idea of being with her as his bear was incredible. She was the one. He was sure of it.

A few minutes later, a slim silhouette emerged from the bathroom. Misty was no longer wearing the dress she wore to dinner. Instead, she was draped in a translucent red robe, the collar and sleeves embroidered with a beautiful crimson lace. Underneath, she was wearing a matching pair of bra and panties in a bright pink. They both hugged her form, accentuating her stunning full breasts and behind. She came back to the couch, walking with the deliberate gait of a supermodel, and Tate couldn't break his gaze from Misty's body. He always imagined her having a slight figure, but he never pictured her looking this good.

"Wow." The word left his mouth as a husky whisper full of lust and need. "Holy shit, you look amazing."

"I thought you'd like it. I've been dying to take it for a test drive since I picked it up. It killed me to break away from our kiss earlier, but I just had to try this on for you. I've never worn anything this sexy before. I've never wanted to."

"It's a shame it's gonna be coming off pretty soon." Tate licked his lips with desire, his cock throbbing in his hand. "Now please get back over here so we can finish what we started."

Misty let the robe fall from her shoulders, pressing her breasts together with her upper arms, while she watched his hand move up and down his shaft.

"God," Tate whispered in a breathy voice and stood.

Misty dropped the robe to the floor. Tate cupped her face, kissing her fully, their mouths opening, and their bodies fell into one another. Her tongue slid between his lips, his tongue teasing hers. He drew her roughly to him, their bodies entwining, and they kissed even more deeply, passion igniting a frenzy in them. Breaking the kiss, Tate slid his hand across Misty's plump thighs and picked her up as if she was as light as a feather.

"I'm going to make love with you." He gasped when she kissed him. With her in his arms, he took long strides to the bedroom. "Because I want you, Misty. I want you so fucking bad."

Misty merely giggled as Tate lumbered to the bedroom, her legs wrapping around his waist for support. He gently placed her on the comforter, her legs open to him and her feet around his lower back.

"If you're going to object," he said, unbuttoning his flannel shirt, "now would be the time to do so. I want to hear you say yes before I go any further. I want to make sure you're ready, and I know once we're in the heat of it, I won't be able to stop. You just turn me on so much."

"Yes." Misty nodded triumphantly. "Yes, Tate, I'm ready."

"Good God, I've been dying to hear those words since the day I met you." He sighed, grinning down at her.

"I'm all yours, all night."

"Then let's get started."

"Tate, please use me. Take me. Make me yours. I want to be owned by your desire, your passion. I'm tired of waiting for it. Please."

He'd never been so hard in his life.

18

Misty

His cock throbbed in her hand, and her wetness became even more apparent, her excitement undeniable. She had to have him inside her. He was huge, fully engorged, and pulsing with each heartbeat. He nuzzled her neck, nibbling, biting, and softly sucking. Moans escaped them, and chills moved through her. Waves of pleasure washed through her again and again.

His mouth burned a line of kisses from her throat across her collarbone, bringing out goose bumps. Her hands moved through his hair, and she arched against his touch, wanting more, craving more. With the fingertips of one hand, he traced the line of her bra while he other teased her through the lace panties with her other hand, and her wetness increased. Slipping her panties aside, he eased his fingers inside and she gasped. With just the right pressure, as he slid his fingers deeper in her, she felt the wave increasing, the pleasure thrumming through her body like a lightning rod.

"God, yes. Please, don't stop. Harder, please. Harder."

His kisses blazed across her breastbone, his tongue flicking her nipple through the fabric of the bra. She wanted his mouth to consume her. His fingers slipped in and out harder and faster, and each time his hand hit her pleasure spot, she gasped, wanting it harder, needing it faster.

"Yes." Her voice was a lusty hushed whisper. She wanted to be his. To be taken whenever he wanted and pleasure him so he didn't crave another ever again.

"Baby, let me feel you come on my hand."

She reached behind her back, unfastening her bra. "I will, baby, if you kiss me right here." He followed her finger with his mouth, kissing her nipples, softly urging her closer with his tongue, his fingers finding a rhythm against her slippery slit, her hips meeting each thrust of his fingers.

As she started to orgasm, she lifted his head from her breast and looked into his eyes. "Tate, God, this is incredible."

"Yes, you are."

She came again and then once more, each one more powerful than the one before. She'd never had multiple orgasms before, but it was impossible not to with his touch. She loved how animalistic he felt moving over her. It was almost like she was in heat— his woman ready to take what he had. She'd never felt anything like it.

Why was this so different?

She unbuttoned his shirt, while he worked on the buttons of his jeans. Her fingers trembled; she could barely get his buttons undone. His body was magnificent. Toned and firm, his chest was hairy just like she'd hoped. His abs were tight and well-formed, and she couldn't help but trace each one as he slipped his jeans off.

She writhed on the bed, his arousal making her drunk with desire, while he stood beside the bed. She stroked him, making him throb even more. He moaned and drew her head toward him. She opened her mouth and took him as deeply as she could. Misty loved feeling his manhood pulse in her mouth. She tightened her lips and suckled, and Tate moaned. She leaned back, releasing him from her mouth with an audible pop, she smiled. He shivered, still hard.

"You're full of surprises tonight," Tate said and kissed her openly on the mouth, pushing her back onto the bed and slid his body over hers.

With her legs open, Tate teased her, touching the tip of his dick to her moistness and then backed off while his kisses ignited her passion even further. He was driving her insane. She wanted him inside her.

"Misty."

She loved hearing him say her name. "Please get inside me. I need it."

"Yes, you do." He trembled with anticipation.

"Are you okay?" she asked playfully, running a finger along his chest.

As he slipped inside her, she gasped and he moaned, burying his face into her hair. His body against hers was too much, and she shuddered against him as another orgasm crashed over her. She'd never come so much before. Then Tate started moving inside her. In and out. Over and over.

They found a rhythm, her hips meeting his with each thrust, and their passion grew. His mouth found her breast again, and she pulled him against her roughly, urging him, craving him, and engulfing his member with her body. Her breath was coming too fast, but her arousal was too much to deny.

Their skin grew slick between them, and their bodies slipped and slid against each other in that delicious way, sweat joining them in impassioned desire, their bodies one, and anticipation gone. There was only each other. Their hands moved over each other, teasing, tasting, and giving.

She didn't want this moment to end. He was so intense, and his thrusts grew more frenzied. He tugged her hair, his mouth against her throat again. Misty locked her legs around his lower back, and he slipped in even deeper and trembled against her.

"Are you ready?" Misty whispered.

Tate nodded, his face slick with sweat, his thick arms drawing her to him.

"Then fill me." Her tone was pleading, wanton, filled with need.

Bursting with desire, he let out a long groan and she felt him pulse three times, and then he finally stopped. Lying together on the bed, breathing hard, they caressed each other until they fell asleep, the sheets tangled around them.

19

Tate

Bacon sizzled in the frying pan, and Tate smiled while looking out the window of the kitchen, the forest alive around the cabin. Misty walked out of the bedroom and into the kitchen.

"Morning."

"Morning," Misty said, giving him a long hug, and kissing his neck.

They'd had sex twice more in the dead of the night. Once, he almost shifted because he was so aroused and was ready to claim her as his mate, but thankfully, he was able to control it. He held her close, his bear wanting nothing more than to continue making love to her, but he knew she needed a break. Tate was going to go for a run to burn off some energy. He knew he had to tell her before they could mate completely. He hoped she didn't shut him out. Tate knew it was a lot to take in.

"I'm going to go for a run before a quick shower," Tate said, kissing Misty, feeling like he'd never getting enough of her petal-soft lips.

"Did you already eat?"

"Yes, did you already forget?" He bumped his eyebrows up and down, and Misty chuckled with him.

"Yes, you did and no, I didn't."

"I'll be back in a bit. I was wondering though..."

"Yes?" She asked took a slice of bacon and wore it as a mustache.

"Cute. Bacon mustaches are so in," Tate said.

"High fashion," Misty said, eating her mustache.

"Yes, indeed." Tate sounded like a stuffy Englishman.

She kissed him, her lips salty from the bacon.

"I've been thinking," he said.

"Oh, boy. Better call Guinness."

"What, the beer?"

"Yeah, the beer needs to know you're thinking. No, I meant the record book guys."

"Oh." Tate smirked.

"You knew what I was talking about."

"Had no idea."

"Shut up."

"You shut up."

"Why don't you make me?" Misty said drawing him in for a deep kiss, her body pressing against his, and his bear fought to get out.

Breaking the kiss, he said, "I'll be right back. Maybe we can meet in the shower?"

Her smile was his only answer.

"Would you like to say up here with me for a few days?"

Misty blinked a few times, still smiling. "Yes. I'd love it. I need to get a few things though. I'll go get them while you're on your run, and we can meet back here."

"Great. God, Misty."

"I know."

They kissed again one more time before they headed out.

20

Misty

The coffee warm between her hands and her stomach full of a wonderful breakfast, she closed her eyes, and her heart swelled with the joy of possibility. Hope was burning bright. Last night was perfect and not just because of the mind-blowing sex but because everything fit. Their conversation. The teasing. The complete and total comfort she felt with him. Whether they were kissing or talking, it didn't matter. He treated her with respect. Misty wasn't a fool. She had felt his desire from the beginning. He had wanted her when they first met, and yet he held to his promise until she was ready.

Handsome and considerate. What a mix.

Getting dressed, she wondered about staying at his place the next few days. Was it a good idea? They'd just met. What if it was a disaster and derailed them because they were pushing too hard to make it happen? She didn't want to lose what they'd had last night. And she didn't want to lose what she felt was relationship with a lot of promise.

Tucking her hair into a messy ponytail, she took one of the baseball caps from a peg in Tate's bedroom. It was a Detroit Tigers hat. She never would've guessed he was a Tigers fan. She shut the door behind her, heading through the woods, eager to start her adventure with Tate.

A short time later, Misty bounced up the steps to the porch and took out her keys. She couldn't believe everything that had happened to her since she'd arrived. How could Amber have been so right about everything?

Stepping inside, she shut the door, her heart so full, happiness swelling her chest. Laughter, thick with malignance and malice, filled her ears.

"Hey, buttercup."

Ice thudded through her veins with each beat of her heart. Lyle was here. With his utterance of two words, he had wiped out her happiness. How had he found her?

"Now, what have you been up to?"

"Lyle."

"So, you do remember my name? How sweet of you. Your phone broken?"

Misty had blocked his number when she'd arrived. She wasn't about to tell him that.

"I bet you're getting back from whoring around, aren't you? I can smell it on you. I'm not stupid."

"You can't be here."

"It's a free country. I can be anywhere I want."

Didn't he just say he wasn't stupid?

"Pretty sure you can't."

"You're actually giving me sass right now? You're talking back to me after what you've done. You have no idea what's waiting for you, babe." Lyle stood up and unbuckled his belt, the leather whispering through the belt loops of his jeans.

21

Tate

His run was almost done, instead of going home, Tate headed to Misty's cabin to see if she needed any help bringing stuff back to his cabin. His steps felt light as he continued to jog. He'd never been happier, loving the fact Misty was going to stay with him. She'd surprised him when she agreed.

The idea of waking up with her beside him stirred his heart like nothing else. He hadn't been with anyone in a long time. It was never a question of wanting to be with someone; it was more that he didn't want to always have to worry about them finding out about his bear. He knew he could never truly be with Misty until he confided in her and told he the truth. Tate didn't want to have any secrets from her.

For the first time ever, he didn't want to keep his secret any longer. He wanted to share it with Misty. She was the one. Tate knew she was special. She was beautiful, witty, and smart. Misty didn't act like she was gorgeous and every man should be checking her out, but she was just that.

His thoughts were a jumble of Misty, so he wasn't paying attention to the sounds coming from the cabin. As he came up the drive, he heard the sounds of a scuffle inside. There were no cars other than Misty's parked out front. What was going on in there?

"Stop it!" Misty yelled.

Her scent was stronger than usual. He knew she was afraid and was in trouble. More yelling was followed by glass breaking inside.

His alarm turned to rage. His canines lengthened, his snout protruded, and his eyes turned a golden hue, his bear taking control. Bounding up the steps to Misty's cabin, he pushed against the door. His immense strength splintered the door, leaving it hanging from one hinge.

Roaring, the sound deafening in the confines of the cabin, Tate's bear was in full form, muscles rippling beneath the thick covering of fur. He felt his rage burning its way to the surface as he swung his paw at the man, knocking him off Misty.

He saw Misty, and something broke loose inside him. She had a bloody lip, and a bruise under her eye was starting to swell. Tate's bear flew into a frenzy; he was no longer able to control it. With animalistic fury, he lost himself in the rage, lunging at the man. He knew instinctively who it was.

It was Lyle.

In mid-lunge, Tate watched the man begin to melt, shimmering a moment like heat coming off a desert highway before transforming into a mountain lion. How could it be? Lyle was a werepanther?

Lyle's werepanther was much faster than Tate anticipated, his claws raking across his underbelly. As he tried to protect himself, the cat sank its teeth into his shoulder. The pain was immediate. His swiping paw too slow, and the cat used its hind legs to kick at his midsection gouging him with its claws once again.

Tate roared again, his bear hurt but unwilling to step aside, his rage still heightened. He couldn't let this piece of crap get to Misty again. He'd die before he let that happen.

"Be careful."

Misty's voice was choked with emotion, and her body was folded up against the overturned couch. Tears marred her cheeks, and her hair was a matted mess. A tiny finger of blood marred her forehead, and he wondered if she had a cut somewhere high up in her scalp.

Lyle attacked again, his cat a feral beast, writhing with unnatural strength, as Tate gripped the animal by the shoulder. He used his claws and finally caught the werepanther high on the chest, red streaks cutting neatly across his chest. It howled, crouched near the family room wall, and hissed at him. Taking a few steps toward the door, Tate's bear blocked his path. There was no way Lyle was going to get away this easy. This was ending now.

"Lyle, if you can hear me, stop this. Stop it!" Misty's voice was filled with heart-wrenching angst, her emotion apparent, and her hands trembled.

The werepanther looked at her, hissing again before turning its attention back to Tate who reared up on his hind legs. At his full height, Tate's bear towered over him, his head brushing across the ceiling, and his growl rattled the windows.

The werepanther launched itself at him. Tate swung his mighty paws and caught the panther in the head, his claws gouging him badly. Hissing, claws lashing out, the mountain lion crashed into the wall before starting to transform back into Lyle, the cat's body shuddering. Shaking his head, the werepanther growled, the sound fierce, rattling deep in his chest, before his fur began to disappear, flesh showing through. It was like watching a magic trick in slow motion, with each passing second more of Lyle appeared.

Misty's eyes were too wide, and the back of her hand was pressed against her lips. She was obviously struggling to make sense of what she had just witnessed. Her mouth hung open, and Tate could smell the fear wafting off her in thick waves. How could he help her to process what she was witnessing?

Instinctively, he stepped toward her, wanting to hold her in his arms. Misty shrieked, holding out her hands as if to ward off an attack, begging him to stop.

She thinks I'm going to attack her.

Tate stood in front of her, frozen in place, and shook his head. His bear form frightened her. Of course, it did. She didn't realize who he was. His heart ached. He just wanted to hold her and comfort her. He looked at his paws with the massive claws jutting out in a menacing way. How was he supposed to comfort her in this way?

Stumbling away from him, she huddled in a corner and sobbed, tears racing down her cheeks. She held out her trembling hands in front of him and rocked back and forth. Tate's heart was crushed by the motion.

Tate took a deep breath, closed his eyes, and centered himself on what was to come next. He relaxed, knowing Misty was watching him. As he opened his eyes, he felt the transformation beginning. His eyes changed color, and his human form began to appear in patches across the body of his bear.

"Oh my God. Tate? This can't be. It just can't."

"Misty, it's okay. It's just me. I know this is crazy. I'm sure it's hard to believe, but it's true. I can transform into a bear. There are people who are werepanthers and change into predator cats like Lyle just did. Have you never seen him change before?"

She just stared at him with a frown on her face and fear in her eyes.

Tate tried stepping toward at her again, but she screamed.

"Okay, okay. Look, it's still me. Nothing is different. I still love you and want to be with you. I was struggling with when to tell you about this. Maybe I should've done it earlier, but I didn't want to scare you away."

"Don't. Don't say that. Get out of here. Leave!" Misty was still trembling, and her eyes grew hard, anger moving through her.

"I'll take Lyle to the hospital. He's hurt pretty bad." Tate picked up Lyle, and the unconscious man groaned in his arms. As he left the cabin, the door closing behind him, he wondered if he would ever see Misty again.

22

Misty

Misty was so shaken to the core, that she couldn't move from the floor for almost a half hour after Tate left. Her sobs finally came under control, and her mind reeled with what she'd witnessed. This had to be a dream. Even though her palms were a mess—raw and red—she kept making a fist and driving her fingernails into her palms to try to wake up. Werepanthers were not real. It wasn't possible. People don't just turn into animals.

Had Tate slipped a drug into one of her drinks? Was she coming down from whatever high he had given her? She didn't think so. He wouldn't do that, would he? He had access to confiscated drugs in the evidence room, but he didn't seem like the kind of person to do something like that. He was too honorable.

When she thought of him, her chest felt constricted, like a giant was squeezing her in his fist. It was hard to breathe. Tate made her feel safe and the passion between them was like nothing she'd ever experienced before.

But he was a bear.

How was any of this normal?

How did it happen?

And how did Lyle find her?

Questions tumbled through her mind, soft bits of dandelion dust moving on the currents of her thoughts. Still shaky, she stood and dried her tears. She had no idea what to do. Misty ached for Tate in her heart and body. She missed him. His strength. His love.

Misty wasn't stupid. She realized she'd thrown a monkey wrench into his life when she'd shown up in town. The first day they met, she could tell he was looking her over. She just hadn't been looking, or she would've known then what she knew now. She loved him.

A weak smile flickered as she heard someone pull up outside.

Had he come back?

She opened the door, but it wasn't Tate and her shoulders slumped. Amber got out of her car with a big smile. She fought to get the suitcase out of the back seat as Misty walked down the porch steps.

Amber grunted. "Could they make the car a little smaller please?"

"Maybe you should pack less."

"Maybe you should shut it." Amber giggled.

Misty smiled. "I'm so glad you're here."

"You sure? You don't look so good. But, don't fret, I have just what the doctor ordered." Amber reached inside her suitcase and pulled out a bottle of wine.

Misty's stomach curled in on itself. The thought of drinking anything alcoholic made her sick to her stomach. "I don't know."

"Oh, come on. You only live once."

Misty nodded, giving Amber a big hug. She could smell the cigarettes on her and wanted to ask what was going on since Amber only smoked when she was really stressed. Misty forgot about her own problems for a moment and wondered if why Amber was so stressed. Maybe things weren't going as well as she'd let on.

"Haven't been up here in a long time. It's still beautiful."

They walk up the porch steps, and Amber gasped. With the door open, it was easy to see the chaos of the inside. The entire place was in disarray. The couch was tipped over, chairs were scattered about, plants were overturned, and dirt and broken glass were strewn across the floor.

"What the hell went on in here, Misty?"

Misty didn't say anything while the two of them stood in the doorway and took stock of the mess.

"It looks like two animals went at it in here."

Misty succumbed to the emotional wave threatening to tug her under. Her eyes itched and her stomach roiled as new tears rolled down her cheeks.

"My God, Misty, please, tell me what's going on? This place is a wreck, and you don't seem yourself. What is this?" Amber dropped her suitcase and put her hands on her hips for a moment before giving Misty a hug.

"Lyle found me."

"Did he hit you again?"

Misty nodded her head, taking a few minutes to get herself under control. All the good feelings, the confidence, and her love for Tate felt like sandpaper rubbing her soul raw. Nothing was what it seemed.

"Amber, you're going to think I'm insane."

"That boat already sailed a long time ago, sister." Amber crossed her eyes and made a silly face.

"I'm not talking about relationship drama. I'm talking like sci-fi channel crazy."

"Oh, please tell me aliens came down and that sexy Fox Mulder guy game to investigate you." Amber put air quotes around investigate for effect.

"Nice. No, nothing like that. Lyle tracked me down, like I said, and he changed into a big cat. Like a mountain lion or something."

"Or something." Amber looked down at her feet, her words muffled.

"What?"

"You never knew. I thought you found out. How did you not find out?"

"Find out what?"

"Lyle's a werepanther. It's what's called his animal side."

"A what?"

"It's a werepanther. It's more common than you think."

Misty scoffed, a laugh that didn't sound a bit like hers sounding flat. "What are you talking about?"

"Misty, I'm one too. It's not a big deal. It's just something I am."

"What are you talking about?"

Amber looked at her pointedly.

Misty's eyes full of laughter, and she waited for Amber to let her in on the joke, but she never did. "Oh, come on." Misty crossed her arms and her jaw dropped. She shook her head. "This can't be happening. Now I know for sure this has to be a dream. No way my best friend and my idiot ex-boyfriend are both werecats."

"Panthers. Werepanthers."

"Oh my God, who gives a were-shit. What the hell is going on?" Misty had finally reached her limit, her anger boiling, and her mind shut down. How was it everyone knew about these things but her? She went to the bedroom and slammed the door.

A few moments later, she stepped into the shower, the water as hot as she could stand it. Trying to wash off the day and slough off the disturbing memories of Tate and Lyle, she lost herself in the suds, her bare body taken over by the torrent of water. She leaned back into the shower head and closed her eyes, the warmth easing her mind and her body.

After drying off, she wrapped a towel around her head and pulled on her robe. When she walked out of the bathroom, she stopped short. How long had she been in the shower?

"Surprise!" Amber said, sitting on the couch that had been overturned and thrown in the corner.

"How did you…"

"Little magic."

"Cat magic?"

"Meow."

Misty laughed softly, walking to the couch, and sat down. She felt much better having showered. Taking a deep breath, Misty puffed out her cheeks as she exhaled. At least she wasn't shaking anymore. She was still unsure about everything.

"Do you want to talk about it?"

Misty gnawed on the inside of her lower lip a moment before nodding. "Yeah, I think I do. I wasn't sure until right now. After hearing you ask the question, it just feels right."

Amber nodded and squeezed Misty's thigh. "Then let's get started."

Misty nodded again.

"I have no idea how long people have been able to do this. There are some people who are shifters, and there are some who are weres like me. I've been able to do it for as long as I can remember. My mom told me when I was five. I changed when I was at a friend's birthday party, which scared the crap out of everyone because they were all human. I couldn't control it the way I can now. We actually had to move twice before my eighth birthday before my mom sent me to live with my father who I get my shifter genes from."

"Amber. I can't imagine." Misty took Amber's hand.

"I'm okay. I wasn't then, but I am now. It was just a secret I had to keep and had to learn not to get too emotional. If I was crying or really angry about something, I had to watch myself so I wouldn't change without meaning to."

Misty thought about growing up as a foster kid and couldn't imagine having to hide such a secret. It would be agonizing.

"Can you show me? I mean your werecat?"

"Werepanther."

"Panther," Misty rolled her eyes playfully.

"I'm not supposed to show humans."

Misty understood. "It's okay."

"No, I can show you. What I was going to say was I can't show anyone I don't implicitly trust."

Misty smiled.

Amber stood and walked to the center of the room. She sat down and put her palms together. Her breathing changed, and Misty sat up a little straighter. Was she okay? She almost said something but stopped when Amber's body shimmered, her muscles rippling as if water churned beneath her skin.

She shifted into her cat. Her fur coat was beautiful, and her eyes were alluring. Misty reached out and touched the cat along the side of its head. The cat began to purr and then meowed softly. Misty knew it was Amber beneath it all and wasn't afraid despite the massive size of the cat. A few moments later, Amber shifted back into her human form.

"It smells like a bear in here."

Misty teared up hearing that. "That's Tate."

"Oh."

Frowning, Misty asked, "What is it?"

"My dad told me about him. We knew he was a shifter too. If there's anyone you can count on in this town, it's him."

Wiping her eyes, Misty sniffed loudly. "This is just so much to handle."

"It's no different than having an allergy or a medical condition. It's not a big deal."

"Easy for you to say."

"Hey, I get it. Kinda like finding out you had a missing twin or you were adopted when you were born on one of those crazy daytime talk shows. But I promise I'm the same person you've come to know, love, and absolutely cherish!" Amber emphasized the word cherish by posing coquettishly.

"Oh, drama much?"

"Oh, definitely drama much." Amber gave her another hug.

"So, what's this I hear about werepanthers liking wine?"

"That was a secret. How did you find out?"

"Well, one of the dopey werepanthers let the cat out of the bag." Misty tried not to laugh but couldn't contain it.

"Really?"

Misty nodded, still laughing.

Amber got up and went over to her bag, pulling out a bottle in each hand. "There's two more in there."

"Well now. What an interesting development."

"Better one?" Amber held out one of the bottles. "Or better two?" She held out the other one.

"Can't we just have both? Why decide? One of the bottles is bound to feel left out if we did it that way." Misty drew a pretend tear down her cheek.

"That's true. It's important to be equal opportunity drinkers so no bottle is left out."

Misty went into the kitchen and opened a few drawers before finding the corkscrew. She handed it to Amber who exchanged one of the bottles of wine for it. Misty reached for some wineglasses in the cupboard above the stove, and Amber opened the first bottle.

"Here we go, madame." Misty held the glasses while Amber poured.

They sat on the couch, each drinking almost their entire glass before talking, and Misty felt relaxed and buzzed. She had an empty stomach, and the wine was hitting her hard.

"I really thought Tate and I had something special."

"You still do. This is just like a creepy ex-girlfriend from his past showing up."

"It's like creepy triplet ex-girlfriends."

"Okay, okay. You're right. But so what?"

"I think I want to see him again, but I'm going to slap him silly and then kiss him like there's no tomorrow." She could tell her speech was getting a little slurred, but she didn't care. She knew how she felt about Tate.

"Good idea. But you should wait and sober up first."

Misty tried to wink at Amber but failed and poured the last of the wine into her glass. "How wise you are, old werepanther friend of mine."

23

Tate

Tate still felt miserable about what had happened at Misty's cabin. It had been a few days, and he still hadn't heard from her. He didn't know if she wanted him to reach out or not.

He wasn't sorry for taking out Lyle the way he had, but he was mortified Misty had to find out about his secret that way. He'd wanted to tell her over a quiet, private dinner at his place, explaining what it meant and its impact on his life. Instead, she saw two mystical creatures in a battle royale in her living room.

He took a moment to write a note to leave on her doorstep. He felt like he was back in high school, leaving a note for a girl in her locker. He was nervous, not sure how she'd take it. Would she be receptive to what he had to say, or had she already closed the door on their relationship?

Misty,

I am so sorry for the other night. I know you must still be in shock over what happened. Are you doing okay? Lyle has been released from the hospital and is awaiting his court date in the jail. I just thought you should know.

What we shared and what we feel for each other means a lot to me. I know it might not seem like it now that you already

*know about my secret, but
I had every intention of
telling you about it. I've
never told another person
about this side of me, but
I trusted you enough to
want to. I hope it's enough
for you to at least talk to
me so we can figure
things out.*

Yours in Bingo,

Tate

Taking a sheriff's department envelope out of his drawer, he looked at it and frowned. He shook his head and dropped it back into the drawer. This wasn't official. He didn't want to tick her off any more than she already was. He'd have to find something more personal.

Walking out of his office, note in hand, he asked Marlene, the secretary, "Do we have any envelopes that aren't quite so official?"

Marlene looked from the folded paper in his hand to his eyes, an odd smirk on her face.

"Passing notes in study hall, Sheriff?"

"Marlene."

"I can hand it to her when she comes out of Spanish just before lunch."

"Marlene."

"Or wait until we're on the bus."

"Marlene!"

She held her hands up a moment before pulling out three envelopes from her middle drawer. "We have an assortment." She fanned out the blue, pink, and dark green envelopes.

"I'll do pink."

Marlene shook her head and slapped his hand away.

"What?"

"Is this an apology for something stupid you've done?"

"Wait a minute. When have I ever done something stupid—"

Her look said it all. He didn't have to finish the question.

"Pink is not an apology color. Pink is an I-want-you-bad color. Blue is a little too cool if you want to have a potential romance after you've apologized for the dumb thing you've done. Green is the 'neutral, no expectations, please read my sad attempt at an apology note' color."

He shook his head, mouth ajar. "Is there a code book or something I can buy in a bookstore, or how about a website where it has all these secrets?"

"Oh, it's all me, baby."

"So, a book full of Marlenisms."

"I like it. I'll have to put that little thought in my bank for later."

She handed him the green envelope. Sheepishly, he took it and headed out the door before she told him the clothes, he was wearing weren't conducive to an apology either.

After a short ten-minute drive, he was at Misty's cabin. After getting out of his truck, he stood and stared at the cabin. He could tell she wasn't there. He picked up another werepanther scent. Worried it might be more of Lyle's pack, he sniffed again. It was female.

He walked up the steps and tucked the note between the edge of the door and the frame. He felt better having left the note, but he wished he could've seen Misty again to make sure she was doing okay. Tate hated not knowing how she was. He returned to his truck and headed back to town.

Driving through the heart of town, he saw Misty and another woman having coffee outside of The Bean, a small shop owned by Delbert Jenkins. He wondered if that was the female werepanther he had noticed earlier.

24

Misty

The coffee was good, and it chased off the chill of the morning. Misty had felt so much better being outside and walking around town. She'd shut herself away after Lyle's attack. Granted, she was wearing oversized sunglasses to cover the bruises and cuts, but no one seemed to pay attention to her.

"Want to get some lunch?" Misty dabbed her lips with the napkin and pushed her empty mug to the center of the table.

"Sure. What's the best this town has to offer?"

"Well, it's not New York City by any stretch, but it's really good."

They walked a few blocks before Misty pointed to the sign for Jack's.

"Jack's?"

"Don't let the sign fool you. It's good stuff. Tate took me there the other night."

"Did he now?"

"Stop it."

They walked into the restaurant and found Jack behind the bar. He waved to Misty.

"Jack, how are you doing?"

"Little better looking than the last time you saw me."

She didn't understand, until he pointed to his hair. He'd just had it cut.

Nice. This is my friend Amber. Amber, this is the aforementioned, Jack."

"Good to meet you." Amber ignored Jack's extended hand and went in for the hug. Men always fell for her when she did that. By the look on Jack's face, Amber had snared another one.

"You two want some lunch?"

"Sure, I'll have the club and fries with a Coke." Misty looked at Amber who hadn't taken her eyes off Jack. She lightly kicked Amber in the ankle to get her attention.

"What?"

"Uh, he wants to know if you want anything."

"Oh, really?" Amber said, almost purring with seduction.

"To eat, Amber. To eat. Sustenance. Food."

"Oh, oh. Okay. I'll have what she's having."

"Be right back, ladies." Jack walked into the kitchen, the swinging door closing behind him.

"Can you be any more obvious?" Misty chuckled.

"He's a yummy mountain man. I have to at least get something out of this lame trip."

"I thought hanging out with me was enough of a reason to come."

"Well, sweetie, you don't compare to being ravaged by a real man."

The two went over to a booth with a view of the street.

"Besides, he's one."

"One what?"

Amber looked around to make sure no one was listening in on their conversation before she whispered, "a werepanther."

"Are you serious?" Misty looked toward the kitchen.

Amber nodded. "Yeah."

Jack brough their plates and set them down on the table, and a young waitress set their Cokes down. "Anything else you need, don't hesitate to ask." He winked at Amber who played coy and unwrapped her straw before slowly drawing the Coke to her mouth, her eyes never leaving Jack. Misty was pretty sure he shivered before walking back to the bar.

They ate in silence, and a few more customers came in for lunch. She looked outside and smiled. It wasn't a place she would've picked to live two years ago but now it looked a little like heaven. She wondered about a job and finding a more permanent place to stay.

As they finished their lunch, Misty said, "Amber, I'm going to run a quick errand. I figured you might want to stick here and do your werepanther mating ritual with Jack."

Amber giggled and finished her Coke. "You know me too well."

"On that note, I'm going to head out. I'll be back in a few so you won't have time to do anything."

"Werepanthers are like rabbits when mating. Quick and dirty."

Misty rolled her eyes dramatically and stood.

Jack walked over and asked, "How was everything?"

"Good as always, Jack. I have to run an errand or two. You mind keeping Amber company?"

He looked at Amber and smiled.

"After all, she is a city girl out in the great Wyoming wilds."

"I'd be glad to." Jack started to clear the table.

"I'll be back." They didn't hear her, too enamored with each other to pay her any mind.

Misty walked north two blocks and up the steps to the police station. She really wanted to see Tate, but he wasn't there.

Marlene, the secretary, had an odd look on her face when Misty asked to talk to Tate. Had Tate told her about what had happened? Did she know about the two of them?

"I'm sorry, honey, but he's not in."

"Can you make sure he gets this?" Misty handed her the note she'd put into a green envelope. The only other envelope she had was pink, and she wasn't about to put her note in a pink envelope.

"Sure, honey." Marlene smiled and stood

Misty left and headed back to her cabin for a few things before picking Amber up. She figured Amber and Jack still needed a bit of time to finish their activities anyway.

Pulling into her parking spot, Misty looked at the cabin. Maybe it was good enough for a permanent place to stay. It was close enough to Tate. Heat rushed between her legs, and she smiled.

When she opened the door, someone grabbed her from behind and flung her to the ground. "Bitch. How dare you fuck some other animal. You're mine!"

Lyle dragged her by the hair over the rocky ground surrounding the cabin. Once they were behind the cabin she saw his truck.

"Help me!" Misty screamed.

Lyle backhanded her hard enough that stars exploded in her vision. She felt like she was going to pass out, but when she saw the cage in the bed of his truck, she knew she had to fight it.

"No! No! You can't do this."

"I don't think you understand the situation. You're mine and always will be no matter who you sleep with. I own you and there's nothing you can do about it."

She kicked him in the knee as hard as she could. His leg buckled, but his grip never wavered. His intent was clear, his eyes burning with it. He smacked her again, and stars exploded across her vision again.

Grinning, he kissed her violently, not letting her pull away. "This is going to be fun."

Evil dripped from every word, his true self finally showing itself. How had she missed it? How had she failed to notice how cruel he was?

He yanked her down to her knees and tugged her hair, and she stumbled to the ground. Taking out a rag from his pocket, he held it over her mouth and nose. She tried to hold her breath as long as she could, and when she couldn't fight him off any longer, she succumbed to the fumes, darkness taking her into its arms.

25

Tate

Tate asked, "Are you kidding me?"

Marlene snapping her gum. "I'm not making it up, dumbass. She was just here probably ten minutes ago."

"What did she say?"

"She said she broke up with Jimmy, the quarterback."

He frowned.

"What? She's not into the jock type. She wants to give the ugly guy a chance."

"Marlene?"

"Yes, Supreme Police Captain?"

"One of these days, I'm going to find me a real secretary."

"She won't be as fantastic as I am," Marlene said, taking the flat of her hand and bumping up her hair.

Tate smiled. He couldn't help it. And he couldn't fire Marlene. She was a godsend.

As he headed for the door, Marlene said, "Go get her, tiger."

If she only knew. He chuckled and climbed into his truck. He sped toward her cabin. Tate couldn't wait to see her. He'd read her note three times.

Tate,

*I'm sorry it's taken me this
long to contact you. I've
had a lot to think about
and to sort out. And,
although I don't have it all
figured out just yet, I know
one thing.*

I want to be with you.

*No matter what you are or
what you aren't, I want to
feel those arms around
me. I want to know what
it's like to be completely
taken again. I long for
your touch, your love,
your everything.*

*Love in Bingo (I won,
remember?)*

M

Driving a bit too fast, he made his way up the mountain in near-record time but slammed on the brakes when he pulled up in front of her cabin and saw her car door open with Misty nowhere in sight.

Why would her door be left like that?

Picking up the handset from his CB, he radioed the jail. "This is Tate. Anyone on, come back."

"Sheriff, this is Dustin."

"Dustin, our prisoner still locked up?"

"Lyle?"

"Yes."

"That's the thing, Sheriff. He just fought his way through four of us and escaped. I have a chipped tooth, and Rogers has a broken nose. I think—"

"Put out an APB for his pickup truck."

"Yes, sir."

"Tate out."

"Dustin out."

His bear struggled for control, but now was not a good time for an appearance. He looked down to the highway and noticed a pickup truck with a tarp over the back. Grabbing the binoculars, he zoomed in on the driver. It was definitely Lyle. What had he done to Misty?

Racing down the mountain path, he pulled onto the highway with screeching tires and wary glances from other drivers. "Marlene, this is Tate." He pushed the truck over eighty.

"This is Marlene."

"Can you put out an APB on—"

"Already have one out after Dustin called."

"Excellent. He's heading north on eighty-one right now. Please let the department know he has Misty. He's kidnapped her."

"Oh no." Marlene paused a moment. "I'll forward the info."

"Thanks, Marlene."

"Watch yourself, Tate."

"Will do."

Lyle's truck weaved in out of traffic dangerously, and Tate hit the lights and sirens The idiot sped up, the tarp flapping in the wind, and Tate saw a cage under the tarp. As he closed in on the truck, he saw someone's fingers holding on to one of the cage's bars.

It had to be Misty.

The traffic parted for him, and he closed the distance, his bear eager to make an appearance. "Not yet. Not yet."

Lyle's truck was no match for Tate's Bronco. He pulled up alongside, Lyle's truck. Picking up the handset and setting it for the loudspeakers atop the cab, Tate said, "Lyle, you've already made one mistake. Don't make another. Pull over. End this now!"

The truck's engine was laboring, but Lyle pushed it a little harder. He rolled the window down and flipped Tate off. Tate roared, his inner bear making an appearance, and with a smug look on his face, Lyle just laughed.

Tate yelled again, "Pull over. Lyle it's done. Shut this down now." Pulling his pistol out, he aimed it at Lyle who just laughed at him.

"Go ahead lawman. Do it and she's dead. This is an out-of-control locomotive if you shoot me."

Tate had no choice. He slowed just a bit and aimed at the tires. He prayed this would work. Gently squeezing the trigger, he blew out both rear tires, pieces of rubber dancing all over the highway as the tires disintegrated. The damage forced Lyle off to the shoulder.

The truck had barely stopped when Lyle jumped out, changed into his werepanther, and roared. Tate changed into his bear and answered Lyle's charge with one of his own. Lyle raked his claws across Tate, slicing into his belly, but Tate didn't stop, his rage unleashed. His claws stabbed through the cat's upper thigh, and the panther shrieked. Spinning savagely, Tate hit Lyle in the side of the head, sending the cat sprawling. Once unconscious, Lyle began to shift back to his human form.

Tate changed back and handcuffed Lyle to the truck before rushing to unlatch the cage. Misty was unconscious and battered. New bruises were all over her arms and legs, but she didn't wake up as Tate put her in the back of his cruiser or when he radioed for help.

26

Misty

Her head pounding with pain, Misty winced against the bright lights above her bed. She looked around her. She was in a hospital room, and Amber was sitting in a chair nearby. Memories flooded through her mind.

Amber almost tumbled out of her chair. "Oh, Misty. Are you okay?"

Nodding, she started to tremble, her emotions getting the best of her. Amber stood and came toward the bed, but Misty waved her off.

"No, no. I'm okay. Just need a couple of deep breaths."

"Do you need anything?"

Biting her lower lip, she looked at her friend and smiled. "Tate. I need Tate."

"He's been here the whole time."

"I'm here," Tate said, stepping into the doorway.

"Tate." Her eyes shimmered with tears.

"It's okay. You're safe now."

"That's not why I'm crying or trying not to cry. I'm so sorry for how I reacted when I saw you in your bear form. I should've been more understanding. I've missed you so much."

"I've missed you too." Tate's eyes shimmered too, and he sniffed loudly.

"Are you a teddy bear now?" Misty laughed uneasily.

"Not quite. My inner bear wants you to know he's much tougher than I am."

They shared a laugh. "Did you need anything?"

Nodding, she whispered, "You. Just you. Take me out of here and let's be together. I need you now."

"Are you sure?"

She reached for him, grabbing a handful of Tate's shirt, pulling him closer. She kissed him deeply, their mouths opening and tongues moving together in a passionate dance. Misty loved him. It was an absolute surety.

27

Tate

Tate gently washed away her cuts and scrapes before getting into the tub with her and helping her with a long hot bath. She was beautiful, her body glistening with the water. He was fully engorged, desperate to be inside her again, to take her, and to mark her as his.

Sounding as desperate as he felt, Misty laid her head back on his shoulder and said, "Tate, please, I need you inside me." She reached behind her and gripped his member firmly in her grasp and stroked him until he was throbbing.

Tate pressed his hand over her sex and moved it in circular motions drawing out moans of pleasure from Misty's lips. "You know what this means, my love? The next time we have sex, you are my mate. Are you sure you want this?"

"I want it. All of it. All of you. Give me everything."

Tate struggled to control his inner bear, his energy fierce and his desire strong. Across his muscular shoulders and chest, sections of his body rippled with fur and then turned back to flesh. Misty's moans aroused him even more.

"You are my mate, Misty. My everything. I can't hold anything back anymore." His voice was lathered with desire.

"I've never felt anything so big." She turned to look at his hardened member. "Why is it so much bigger now?"

"It's my inner bear. He's satisfied you've agreed to be my mate. When he's this sated, he shows it by this."

"Please, I want you inside me." Her eyes danced as she ran her fingers through his chest hair which had thickened. "I want more of this." Misty giggled, the sound like honey dribbled across his soul.

He didn't want to wait any longer. As he stood, he scooped Misty up and carried her to their bed and placed her gently on her back and laid down on top of her. Pushing his hips forward, the head of his throbbing cock bumped against her wetness. Spreading her legs farther, he struggled a moment longer before slipping inside. So was so tight and snug he wasn't going to last very long. He slipped in and out of her, and they grunted and groaned along with the waves of pleasure.

Teeth bared, Tate roared, and his fangs lengthening, looking down at Misty who nodded. She knew what he needed to do.

"It might hurt a little when I mark you," Tate said in a voice mixed with his inner bear. "It's to let other shifters know you've been taken by me. That way, they'll keep their distance."

"It's ok, baby. I want it to hurt a little. I'd love you to mark me. I want to be yours."

Tate felt contentment rushing through him, and he and his inner bear joined as one. His arms, shoulders, and chest grew a bit hairier, his cock swelled a bit more, and his movements grew more intense with the need to mate.

Turning her head, he sank his teeth into the crook of her neck, biting her. When he tasted her skin and blood, he started bucking and she screamed. He could sense that her scream wasn't from pain, but from pleasure and that aroused him even further. She nodded to him as he released his bite and they both came, his cock spurting inside of her, marking her as his. Amber cried out her release along with him as they orgasmed in concert, the thrumming pleasure palpable.

"I want you to have my cubs," he said as he kissed her lips passionately. Their tongues dueled and he continued to rock himself inside her slowly.

"Yes," she said between breaths. "I want to have your cubs."

It was more than he wanted to hear. Tate rocked his hips as Misty wrapped her legs around him and moved her hips to meet his thrusts.

"Don't stop," she cried out once more before she came again around him.

Tate increased his speed not wanting to stop, her words more like a command. With a few more thrusts, Tate roared as a blissful wave rolled through him. Feeling sated, he rolled over onto his side, slipping from her tightness.

Misty rolled over onto her side and hooked a leg over one of Tate's. "Can we stay like this? Just the two of us for a few days? I can't seem to get enough of you and your bear."

He nodded, desperate to be inside her again.

28

Six Months Later

Misty

Misty sat on the bench watching Tate chop wood. His muscles rippled with each stroke of the ax. She was turned on simply watching him, and she rubbed herself through her dress, feeling the tickle of wetness already starting.

"Amber wanted to know if she and Jack could come up for dinner."

"Tonight?" Tate asked, not stopping, continuing to chop wood with a flurry of motion.

"I told her maybe in a week."

"That's my girl."

He split another log, the ax head biting into the wood neatly. She rubbed her neck where he had bitten her. Misty loved the feeling of her scar beneath her fingers, the bite marks arousing when she looked at them in the mirror. She would surrender to his every need if he would just continue to do that.

"Lyle is in a lot of trouble," he said.

"I figured," she replied calmly. His name hadn't sparked fear like it used to. Lyle had been in the hospital for a few months before being sent to jail. Misty knew it was a matter of time before she would hear his name being mentioned again.

Tate turned to look at her and said, "Not just with the law. I'm talking about his pack. What he did to you is against their laws too. He's been banished from his pack. They've left the justice and punishment side of things up to me. I contacted them and talked to their leader for some time on the phone. Lyle's going to be in jail for a long time.

"I'm not worried about him anymore."

Tate raised an eyebrow. "You're not?"

"Not since I have this big bad bear around to keep me safe."

She walked down the steps, over to Tate, and rubbed the front of his pants, loving the growing bulge and how fast she aroused him.

Picking her up, Tate put Misty on the porch railing, and he slipped his hands beneath her dress. "No panties. Naughty girl." Finding her wetness, he grinned. "What have you been doing?"

"I've been a little bad."

"I love when you are." Tate slipped his finger inside her, making her gasp. He knew just how to touch her to make her tremble.

"I need you to take me. I want to feel you inside me. Nothing turns me on more than to feel your skin against mine and your thickness stretching me."

"I want you to have my cubs."

"I'm already going to."

He stopped moving his fingers, his face full of surprise. "What do you mean?"

"I'm already pregnant." Tears of happiness welled in her eyes. She still couldn't believe she was going to have a family of her own.

"Really?" he asked, grinning.

Misty nodded. "I peed on three pregnancy sticks just to be sure."

"Baby, you make me so happy." He kissed her deeply before picking her up and carrying her into the house and into their bedroom. "I love you so very much, Misty," he said as he placed her gently on her feet.

"I love you, too, Tate."

Tate helped Misty out of her dress then stepped back to look at her, his eyes stopping to her stomach. "I can't believe I'm going to be a father."

Misty smiled when he knelt and kissed her belly. "You're going to be a wonderful father."

She bit her lip as Tate kissed his way down to the apex of her thighs and moaned as his tongue teased her nether lips, tracing her slit with the tip of his tongue.

"I can taste your honey you're so wet," he said, looking up at her. "Sit on the edge of the bed, baby. I need more."

Throbbing with the need for release, Misty did as he asked. She loved the way he pleased her and eagerly opened her legs. She sucked in a breath as Tate leaned in and kissed the top of her cleanly shaved mound, the tip of his tongue gently brushing her sensitive bud.

"My gosh, Tate. You're going to make me come."

He glanced up at her, "but I've barely touched you."

"You've had me turned on just watching you chop wood."

"Oh, yeah? I have some wood for ya." Tate stood up and quickly pulled his clothes off. "I have all the time in the world to eat your sweet honey. My mate needs something else from me."

Misty whimpered when Tate pushed her to the middle of the bed and sheathed himself inside her. His sweaty body was so delicious and slick against her skin. She spread her legs wider and rocked her hips, working his hard member inside her, gushing as he pushed inside. Their lives together were destined to be incredible. She could see it all as he ravaged her, nibbling on that sweet spot at the crook of her neck, and they trembled against one another as they rode that blissful wave together.

Her tears came from pleasure and from happiness. She knew they would never part, never stop loving each other, and never end the pleasure they felt when they were together.

She closed her eyes, perfection between her legs, love in her heart, and her mate in her arms.

Epilogue

Eight Months Later

Tate

He had never been happier, and he loved sharing himself with Misty. Tate had never felt such an overwhelming sense of finally being complete. Emotionally, physically, and spiritually. He felt completely connected to Misty. Every fiber of his being and his inner bear were tantalized with her.

Candles gently flickered, and the room was full of the scent of jasmine. Misty had been glowing with that beautiful maternal light in her skin and joy in her eyes for weeks. When her hands cradled her growing belly, all he could do was smile. There was absolute joy here.

He had called Maggie, Jack's aunt, who was the pack's matriarch and local midwife, to help with the delivery. They had called her the day after Misty told Tate that she was pregnant. Jack brought Tate a celebratory bottle of scotch to congratulate him and Misty on their joyous news, and another one a few months later when they learned that they were expecting twins.

Amber walked past and gave his arm a squeeze. Misty had wanted her at the delivery too.

"It won't be too long now," Amber said.

"That's right. Contractions are right on schedule." Maggie's mostly gray hair was pulled back in a severe bun, her glasses perched precariously on the end of her nose. She had washed her hands and placed towels and a bowl of water beside the bed.

It looked like it was time.

Misty was lying in the bed. Sweat coated her face, and a damp rag was on her forehead. The babies were on the way. She smiled at him and nodded.

"Are you ready?" Tate asked, his bear's contented growl coating his words. He moved the damp rag and kissed Misty's forehead.

"I am." Misty squeezed his hand for a moment.

Maggie had been keeping track of the contractions, which had been slowly increasing in intensity. "Then push and count to five."

She did as Maggie asked, groaning with the pain. He could see the head of the cub crowning, more showing with each heartbeat.

"Almost here." Amber readied the towels.

"She's right, Misty. One more push for that first cub. Let's try again and count to five."

Groaning again, she pushed, and the baby slipped out into Maggie's hands.

Amber took the baby from Maggie and wiped off the afterbirth. "We have a boy," Amber said, smiling. She was beaming almost as much as Misty was.

He was beautiful. His son was glorious to behold. His emotions raging inside, Tate struggled to stay in control for Misty. She needed his strength and his comfort.

"The second one is on the way," Maggie said, washing her hands as she prepared to deliver their daughter.

"I don't know if I'm ready. I'm so tired." She sounded out of breath.

"One more, baby. You can do it." Tate kissed her on the forehead again and stroked her hair, his hand still in hers.

The candle light flickered over them as she pushed once more.

"Let's try and push and count again. Let's take it to five again." Maggie's voice was soothing, a permeating calm through every word.

It took two more pushes, each one taking more out of Misty. Tate did his best to hold her and help her through it.

"Here she is," Amber said, taking the tiny female baby from Maggie, cleaning her, and wrapping her in a fresh towel.

Tate wiped Misty's brow and gave her more ice chips. He softly kissed her on the cheek. "I love you."

She smiled at him. "I know you do. I love you too."

Misty and Amber held out the twin babies to them. Tate handed the girl to Misty and held the boy to his chest before lying beside Misty and his daughter in the very bed his children had been born in.

"What a truly beautiful family," Maggie said.

Amber bent down and kissed Misty's cheek. "Why don't we go in the next room and give them a little time alone."

Maggie nodded. "Sounds good to me."

Once they stepped out, Amber closed the door behind them, and Tate basked in the momentous occasion. How had he been so lucky, so blessed?

"You've made me so happy." Tate watched as Misty nuzzled their daughter, his son shifting in his arms.

His bear finally at rest, content and happy, Tate realized for the first time in his life he was truly happy.

About J. Raven Wilde

J. Raven had spent most of her life traveling around the US or abroad, managing to find a bookstore in every city she visited. She began writing when she was a little girl, and it slowly grew into something she loved doing.

Now that she isn't traveling as much anymore, she spends her time writing steamy romance stories at her quiet modest home by the lake.

Connect with J. Raven Wilde

If you loved this story, sign up to receive J. Raven's newsletter at www.TwistedCrowPress.com. Subscribers get the latest information on cover reveals, new or upcoming releases, and promos. Plus, it's FREE, and she promises never to spam you or give out your information. You can also follow her on her Facebook Group, Wilde Raven's Steamy Reads.